THE ----
HISTORY
-- OF US

NYRAE DAWN

Harmony Ink

Published by
HARMONY INK PRESS

5032 Capital Circle SW, Suite 2, PMB# 279, Tallahassee, FL 32305-7886 USA
publisher@harmonyinkpress.com • http://harmonyinkpress.com

The History of Us
© 2015 Nyrae Dawn.

Cover Art
© 2015 Aaron Anderson.
aaronbydesign55@gmail.com
Cover content is for illustrative purposes only and any person depicted on the cover is a model.

ISBN: 978-1-63476-179-6
Digital ISBN: 978-1-63476-181-9
Library of Congress Control Number: 2015933432
First Edition June 2015

Printed in the United States of America
∞
This paper meets the requirements of
ANSI/NISO Z39.48-1992 (Permanence of Paper).

To Jamie Manning. You are such a kind, gentle, helpful soul. Thank you for all that you do. I'm honored to call you a friend.

Acknowledgments

I couldn't do what I do without the love and support of my family. They stick by me, even when I'm in crazy-writer mode. Thank you. I love you. Being a writer can be a lonely journey. Without my closest friends, I'm not sure I could deal with it: Wendy Higgins, Kelley York, Jolene Perry, Steph Campbell, Christa Desir, and Julie Prestsater—you guys are my rocks. Love you all. Thank you to Allie Brennan and Heather Young-Nichols for reading early drafts, and for generally being awesome. My agent, Jane Dystel for everything you've done for me. Lastly, I'd like to thank everyone at Dreamspinner/Harmony Ink. Thank you for taking a chance on me and for believing in this story as much as I do.

Chapter 1

"COLLINS, DID you hear me, man? What the fuck? You're totally spacing out over there." Chase throws a napkin at me and everyone at our table laughs. I pick it up and toss it back at him, making it bounce off his forehead. Before he can grab it again, Marcus jerks it off the table.

"Are you ladies done? We're trying to plan a night out here." Jabbar shakes his head. His real name is Frankie, but most of the time we call him Jabbar because he's tall as hell and holds the scoring record for our basketball team. His 63-point game isn't as good as Kareem Abdul-Jabbar's, but to us it is. He's a basketball legend at our school.

We live and breathe basketball. We always have. The four of us have been starters since we came into high school four years ago— Jabbar at center, Chase the power forward, Marcus the shooting guard, and me at point. I've been friends with these guys since we were in kindergarten, and we've been playing just as long.

Before any of us can reply, I notice Marcus nudge Chase from his seat beside him. As soon as Chase's eyes light up I know exactly what he sees. Or who.

Girls.

Fuck.

"Holy shit, they're hot. Come on. Let's go talk to them." Chase's tongue is practically hanging out of his head. Jabbar turns around and looks. I see his radar going off too. He wants to go over there just as badly as the rest of them do. Whatever Chase was talking about before is lost in the possibility of kissing and tits.

I knew there was a reason I didn't feel like coming to The Spot tonight. It's the arcade/coffeehouse where everyone at our school hangs out. Whoever thought of it is a fucking genius, getting us hopped up on caffeine and then putting bright, flashy games in front of us. We can't get enough. There's an added bonus that adults avoid The Spot like it has a restraining order against them—just the way we like it.

Jabbar's eyes finally leave the girls and then land on me. I avoid his gaze for a second, looking back at the group of four girls. Of course there would have to be four, and in that second, I wish I could be into them. Wish I would see in the girls what the others do, or feel the same things when I look at them. It would make my life a whole lot easier.

Jabbar glances at me. "Nah, let's just chill," he says.

"Yeah," Marcus agrees, and takes a drink of his coffee, but I'm already shaking my head.

"Screw that. You guys aren't staying behind because of me." It's cool that they want to, but it still makes my lunch try to crawl up my throat. I'm not holding them back from doing what they want to do.

"You sure, Bradley?" Chase asks, but he's already starting to stand up. I get out of the bench seat so Jabbar can go too.

"Yeah, yeah. It's cool."

They don't ask me to go with them anymore, which is good. Going made things a whole lot more awkward anyway. It made me feel like I was wearing a sign, or something—"I'm the gay friend. Don't try to hit on me." It's not much better than what I imagine their excuse is for why I don't go with them—why there are four girls but only three guys since I hang back. *Yeah, our boy's into boys. He's cool, though.*

And they're chill most of the time as well. It was one of my biggest fears when I came out—how would my friends take it? Yeah, we've known each other since we were young, but a lot of the time, that doesn't matter.

Kicking my feet up on the bench across from me, I pick up a straw wrapper and start twisting it around my finger. I'm lucky. I know I am. My sophomore year I came out to my mom. Apparently she already knew. She could have saved me a whole lot of stress if she'd have let me in on that fact.

When I got sick of making up excuses as to why I never wanted to hook up, I told my friends my junior year. Everyone at school knows, and no one's given me shit. I get how lucky that makes me. Not everyone has had it as easy, but that doesn't mean I don't feel like punching something because I'm sitting here by myself and they're all at another table trying to get laid. Oh, and *they've* all been laid. I haven't.

There are zero gay people in my family. Zero gay people in my school, who are out about it, at least. They could be there and hiding. I actually *know* zero gay people at all. Mom's always trying to talk me into going to this LGBT teen group she found in Brownsville. It's only about forty-five minutes away, but it's not like I need any other friends.

I have my own. Who gives a shit if none of them are gay? I don't see the point in making a big deal out of my sexual orientation.

I ball the wrapper up and toss it to the table before I let my gaze travel to the other side of the room, trying to find what had me distracted when Chase was talking to me earlier.

Crap. There's a girl and a guy sitting at the table the black-haired guy had been at. I shake my head and grab my cell phone. It's not like it should matter anyway. Still, my eyes sort of case the room. I wonder if he took off or just moved somewhere else. I've seen him in here before, doing whatever he does on his laptop all the time, though I don't recognize him from our school.

"Hey," a voice says to my left. I look over to see it's laptop guy and scramble up from my slouched position.

"Hey." *Why are you talking to me?*

"How come you didn't go talk to the girls with your friends?" He nods back to where the guys are. His hair is spiked. From there I look down, taking in the rest of him. His T-shirt is on inside out, but I can still tell his clothes are expensive.

"Umm, who are you? And why does it matter? Maybe I just didn't feel like it." Really, I know why it matters. I saw him in here with a guy about four months ago. Maybe that's why I always notice him, even though we've never spoken a word to each other—because he's gay too.

"I'm TJ." He pushes his laptop strap up his shoulder and holds out his hand.

Reaching out, I shake it. The heat from his hand slowly slides up my arm, reminding me of a movie or something, when people meet someone and say they feel it. It almost seems like he can see my reaction, so I jerk my hand back.

TJ smiles. "Do I get your name?"

"Bradley." I cross my arms, wishing I could shake out the burn still there.

"Can I sit?" he asks.

"Why?" pops out of my mouth. That doesn't stop a vision from drifting through my head—what it would be like to sit with a guy like him while my friends are off doing their thing.

TJ's brows draw together, and I notice his eyes are blue, this really bright, vivid blue.

"Are you gay?" TJ asks. "I mean, I thought because I've seen you staring at me, but—"

"Shh." My eyes dart around to see if anyone heard him. When they find TJ again, there's a tightness in his jaw that wasn't there before. Guilt makes my stomach drop, like a ball falling through the basket—nothing but net. "I just...." *I've never had someone know without me telling them.* In case you're wondering, my mom doesn't count.

"Fuck yeah. That was awesome—oh, hey, man, what's up?" Marcus says as my three friends step up to us.

"Hey," TJ says to them.

I see my friends look at him, and then look at me, before looking at TJ again. Maybe it sounds stupid, but if Marcus's skin weren't so dark, I swear it would be red right now. Jabbar plops down on the seat across from me like he still hasn't put two and two together. He doesn't realize that for the first time a guy is talking to me with maybe the same thing in his mind that they have when they hit on girls. He rubs a hand over his buzzed, blond head. "They were hot, Bradley. You don't know what you're missing out on."

TJ's frown gets deeper, but it's Chase who speaks, looking at TJ with his forehead wrinkled, like he doesn't belong. "Collins, let's go. I need you to give me a ride home."

I'm already to my feet when Jabbar says, "I'm chillin'. Wanna stay, Marcus?"

He takes the seat I just left. Chase puts an arm around my shoulders. My stomach still feels like it's going through the net.

"I'll play you a game of one-on-one when we get to my house. You down?" Chase starts walking, and I automatically start doing the same.

"Yeah. Sure. Let's do it."

It's not till I get to the door that I sneak a look over my shoulder. TJ is standing by the table where I left him, his hard stare following me as I go.

"Come on." Chase tugs on me, and I keep going.

He screws around on his phone for most of the drive home. We ride together for almost everything because we live next door to each other and I have my own car. Since it's just me, Mom, and my little brother Tyson, she wanted me to have my own way of getting around, which really means she wanted me to be able to help her get Tyson around. I get it. She's a nurse at the hospital and works twelve-hour shifts. It makes things tough for her. Plus, having my own car definitely works for me.

When we get out in my driveway, I ask him, "We gonna play?"

He shakes his head. "That cool? It's cold. I just feel like going inside and chillin'."

Which isn't really like Chase, but what am I supposed to say? "No problem. I'll see you in the morning."

I make it a couple steps away from him when he says, "Hey, Collins. That guy, was he, like, hitting on you or whatever?"

No. Yes. I don't know. I think so. How am I supposed to know? "No."

"I mean, it's cool. You know it's cool. We all know, and if anyone gives you shit, they'd have to deal with all of us, it's just.... We've never really seen you.... You always just hang with us.... You don't ever...." I'm pretty sure this is only the second time in his life he hasn't known what to say, and the first is when I told him I'm gay.

Chase is my best friend. We're all close, but he's always been my boy, so I know exactly what he's saying. "I know. It wasn't like that." *But it could be. Maybe it should be. What happens when one day it is?* The thought makes my skin prick with unease, so I shake it from my head.

"I know it'll happen, but it just might... does it make me a dick if it's kind of weird? I know you're gay, but you've never had a boyfriend, or whatever. It's just... different."

No one really wants to be different. I don't care what they say.

"No. It's cool. I get it. It wasn't like that," I say again. The thing is, I really *do* get it. Chase's worried it makes him a jerk to think like that, but what does it make me? What does it mean that I know I'm gay, yet I don't know how to really *be* gay? I don't know how to be the guy who has a boyfriend when everyone I hang out with has a girlfriend. That I'd rather get left behind at The Spot or stay home when they go out, than to sit with a guy like TJ in a busy restaurant and admit that he could have been hitting on me.

No matter how wrong I know that is, I still can't change how I feel.

Chapter 2

I'M SITTING at home the next Friday night when someone knocks on my bedroom door. Mom is the only option because Tyson is a douche most of the time, and he'd just bust in.

"Yeah?"

The door creaks when she pushes it open. She's wearing her scrubs, having just gotten off work. "What ya up to?" She sits on my bed, where I'm lying down playing a game on my phone. Her brown hair falls forward, and she pushes it behind her ear. It's the same light shade as mine.

"Nothing."

"I'm going to bring your brother to a friend's house. Are you and the guys doing anything tonight?"

I shake my head, wondering if she has some sort of freaky superpower or something. She always asks me questions I don't want to answer. "Nope."

"Why?" There's no reason for her to ask when she already knows.

"Because I don't feel like it." Totally a lie. I'm bored out of my mind, but they're going out with the girls they met last week.

Mom sighs. "Bradley, I know they're your friends, and it's great, but I hate that you stay home waiting for them when you can't go out with them. It's okay to meet other friends too, you know. You should go to the center we talked about. It'll be good for you. I can go with, if you want."

I laugh at that and then sit up to lean against the headboard of my bed. There's not one person I can think of who would want to go to some kind of youth group with their mom. "Can we not do this for the ten thousandth time? I don't need to go there. I don't want to." When I can tell she's not convinced, I add, "I don't feel like going out with the guys anyway. We're hanging out tomorrow."

"Which is a good thing, but they don't have to be your only friends, sweetheart. I think it'll help to be around more kids like you."

I pull away from her, and push to my feet. "Like me? Because I'm different than Chase, Jabbar, and Marcus. Nice, Mom."

"Hey." The tone of her voice is sharp. "You know that's not what I meant."

Do I? I'm not sure that I do. Those words get stuck in my throat, though. I know she means well. It's always been just me, Mom, and Tyson. I hate fighting with her. That doesn't stop my muscles from feeling stiff, though. She's always pushing me. "I know." I shove my feet into my Nikes. "I'm gonna go, is that cool? I think the guys are at The Spot. I'll probably go chill with them. They said I could already." The lie comes out smoothly.

"Bradley...."

Crap. She's still not convinced. I walk over and drop a kiss to her forehead. "You're right, Mom, I need to get out. I just... they're my friends. Maybe I can do that other thing some other time." Never going to happen.

There's still doubt in her eyes, but she stands and tells me to have fun.

An hour later I'm still in my car, outside The Spot. The guys aren't here, but I knew that before I showed up. They're in Brownsville at the IMAX theater, but sitting in my car for hours is better than a lecture.

I jump when someone knocks on my passenger side window. When I turn, my eyes lock with TJ's. "What the fuck, man?" I ask after rolling down the window. My face feels hot, and I hope it doesn't look flushed.

"You've been sitting out here forever."

Suddenly, the steering wheel is really interesting because I'm staring at it instead of him when I answer. "You watching me, or what?"

"Says the guy who's been lurking in his car, and who I've caught looking at me more than once in the past."

That makes me snap my head toward him. "I wasn't looking at you."

He shrugs. "Sucks me for me, I guess, because I was looking at you."

My body gets hot all over, and I swear, I'm scared I'm *blushing* or something. But I like what he says. His hair is spiked again, shorter on the sides and in the back than it is on top. His eyes are like lasers shooting through me. I want him to look at me. I like the way he looks. *He likes looking at me too....* And he's not a girl. I can't tell you how many times I've had a girl's eyes on me, had girls ask me out, and it never felt like this.

I don't want it to go away. "Wanna... I don't know... like, go for a ride or something?"

It takes a minute for TJ to reply. "Since your friends aren't here, and no one would know?"

Yes. My hands tighten around the steering wheel. "Fuck you. I'm out. Everyone knows I'm gay." Still the last word is spoken more softly than the others. It makes me feel like a pussy. "Never mind."

I turn the key and TJ says, "Wait. Hold up. I'm coming."

He gets in the car and neither of us speaks. I drive out to the edge of town, which takes about twenty minutes, and pull into the parking lot of a bowling alley. It's old, the paint peeling off. There's a league from the retirement home that plays here, but I'm not sure if anyone else does. Once I get into the parking spot under a light, I kill the engine.

Questions slam around in my head, but I don't let any of them out. This is what I've wanted but never had the balls to admit—to know someone who is gay. To not feel so alone.

"Why do you always have your laptop with you?" I ask.

"I'm editing film. One day I'm going to make movies. I'm always working on something. Why do you always have your friends with you?"

Dude. What is he trying to say with that? "Fuck you."

"You said that already. Plus, I'm kidding. Kind of. They know you're gay?"

Didn't I already say that? "Yeah, everyone does. I came out last year." I set my elbow on the door and lean against it. No matter how hard I try to keep my mouth shut, I ask, "You?"

"When I was fourteen."

"Did your parents, like... care or whatever?"

"Nope. They're really supportive. They're really proud. PFLAG parents all the way."

I have no clue what PFLAG is, but I don't tell him that.

"Did yours care? Is that why you're ashamed?"

My defenses scream at that, my heart kicking up like it's the end of the game and we're down one point. "I'm not ashamed. I don't give a crap what people think. If I was embarrassed, I wouldn't have come out."

"Yeah, okay." TJ looks up at the sky through the windshield, and I wonder what he's seeing out there.

"I'm serious."

"I said okay."

"I'm not stupid. I heard how you said it."

"Listen, I don't mean to be a dick about it. It's just… it's important, ya know? To be proud of who you are. If you aren't, who will be?" This is what I don't want to deal with. It's one of the reasons I don't want to go to the group. Everyone has to make a big event about being gay.

Time to change the subject. "I play basketball. You play any sports?" I ask him.

He frowns but then says, "I used to play more than I do now. I'd rather be making movies, though. I'm doing a documentary for my senior project in film class. The winner gets entered into a national contest. Over spring break I'm going on a road trip and talking to LGBT people of different walks of life… sharing their stories and just kind of studying the history."

Holy crap. I would never have thought of doing something like that, but it's pretty cool. "Where do you go to school? I didn't know any of the high schools around here had film class." Mine doesn't.

"Brice Private School."

I laugh. "Rich, private school kid, huh?"

Heat shoots through me again when TJ looks at me and winks. "Hot, right?"

This time both of us laugh.

For the next three hours we sit in my car and talk. TJ's pretty cool. Not as much of a jerk as I first thought. My sides hurt I've laughed so much.

When I drop him back off at The Spot at eleven thirty, he pauses, not getting out of the car. My pulse starts slam dancing. I've kissed three girls in my life, hoping each time I would like this girl more than the last. I've never kissed a guy. The thought makes me both nauseous and sort of like I just hit a game-winning shot at the same time.

"Gimme your phone," TJ finally says. Without a word, I do it.

He puts in his phone number. Then he dials his so he has my number too. TJ tosses it back to me and then slides out of the car. "You're not so bad, Bradley."

I don't move, don't drive away for a long time after TJ leaves. Excitement blazes through me, but I'm confused as to why. He might not be into me. I'd lose my shit if he were. But I think the excitement is stifling the rest. I just hung out with a guy who might be into me.

The drive from The Spot to my house is only ten minutes, but I still miss my midnight curfew. It's worth Mom yelling at me.

In my dark room that night, I look at TJ's number glowing on the screen of my phone. There's a hope inside me, a newness that's never been there before, and I know I'm going to call him.

Chapter 3

I'VE BEEN meeting with TJ after school, weekends, and whenever I'm not busy or with Chase, Jabbar, and Marcus, for the past two weeks. We don't really do anything. He talks about his documentary a lot. It's cool. I get that kind of passion because I'm the same way about basketball.

He's got this whole plan set up, with different stops in different states. He's going all the way from here to New York. Not that Wisconsin to New York is crazy far, but it's far enough. Nothing's happened. In some ways it's just like being with my friends, but there's that possibility mixed in. I'm still trying to sort through how I feel about that. A few times I've almost felt bad because I haven't told my friends, but then why trip them out if I'm not even sure what's going on? *And I don't know what I'd do if they couldn't handle it either....*

I'm playing a doubles game of pool—me and Chase against Jabbar and Marcus—when I see TJ walk into The Spot. My stomach automatically flips, my shot way off from where I wanted it to go.

"What was that, Collins?" Chase laughs.

"I got tired of carrying you the whole game," I toss back at him.

Both Marcus and Jabbar laugh.

My eyes dart to the door again, and I notice TJ still standing there. A minute later another guy comes in. They walk together to a table and sit down. *What the...?* I mean, not that it matters or anything. But... who is it?

"This is gay. They're going to beat us. Marcus is about to clear the table," Chase groans from beside him.

I've heard people complain about something being *gay* so many times, that it almost feels normal to me now. My friends don't mean anything by it, and they've said it less since I came out to them. The word is just something they say without thinking.

Pulling my attention away from TJ, I respond, "Eh. We have to let them win every once in a while." Chase laughs and we bump fists.

After Marcus and Jabbar kick our ass, we head back to the table.

"So, did Jabbar tell you he's got himself a girl now?" Chase asks.

"Aww, how sweet. Are you in love, man?" I tease him. They might hook up often, but none of them really does the serious girlfriend thing.

Jabbar doesn't answer. We chill for a little while, finishing our drinks. "Hey, what are you doing after this, Collins?" Chase asks me.

Usually when he asks that it's because he wants to come over. His parents are nice and all, but they're always busy and pretty much leave Chase to fend for himself. Mom basically adopted him years ago. He's just as comfortable at my house as I am. "Nothing. Wanna come over for dinner?"

"Sure." He nods, and I know that's a thank-you.

The conversation veers off from there. Everyone continues to talk shit to each other, and talk about school and ball. I keep up my end of the conversation, while at the same time watching TJ.

It seems like kind of an asshole thing to do, for him to show up here with some guy. In reality, I know it's not. I'm not with him, and I don't even talk to him around my friends. Still, I can't help but wonder who the boy with him is, while at the same time flinching every time TJ walks somewhere, worried he'll come this way.

No matter how much I try to pay attention to the guys, my eyes wander back to TJ. Yeah, I know, it's close to stalker territory, but I really don't want to have a repeat of the other day. It's much better being on the side of it where I get to give Jabbar crap about having a serious girlfriend than seeing them uncomfortable because they think I'm into TJ.

"I'm bored. You guys ready to go?" Jabbar asks.

"Got a date with your girl?" Marcus asks.

"So what if I do? What are you guys gonna do tonight?"

Everyone shuts up at that.

We grab our stuff and head toward the door. We're about halfway there when I notice TJ heading toward us with whoever the guy is with him. *Shit.* What kind of crap will they give me if they think something's up with TJ? Hell, Jabbar's getting it just because he actually likes someone. I don't want to hear the wisecracks about a boyfriend. Don't want to see Marcus embarrassed, like he was before.

"What's up?" TJ says when he gets to us. He stops walking, but I try to only slow down.

"Hey."

Jabbar stops, which then makes the rest of the guys stop too, leaving me no choice but to do the same.

"I tried to call you earlier to see if you wanted to hang out. Maybe tomorrow or something?"

My stomach drops out. It's a struggle not to look at Chase or my friends. "I don't know. Listen, we're heading out. Have a good one." Why the hell would TJ say that in front of my friends?

Without waiting for TJ to reply, or my friends to say something, I walk away. My chest feels tight the whole time. My face burns, and I push my legs to move faster. That was such a dick thing for me to do. Everything inside me wants me to go back, but I don't.

I'm halfway through the parking lot when a hand comes down on my shoulder. "Hey." Jabbar spins me around to face him. "Why'd you take off like that? If he's your friend, or if you're, like, seeing him or whatever, it's cool."

"Aww, our little boy's growing up. Bradley has his first boyfriend." Chase laughs. "Finally you're going to get some." But I can see unease in his eyes—see that, just like the other night, he's a little weirded out by the thought.

I don't want to be different. Don't want my best friend uncomfortable. I want to know who that guy was with TJ. Maybe he's dating him. Maybe he's not into me at all.

My hand shoots out, and I push my best friend. "Fuck off, Chase."

He stumbles backward. "What the hell, B? I was kidding."

"It's not funny."

"Oh, so you can talk shit to Jabbar and the rest of us, but no one can do it to you? Stop being such a pussy."

It's that last word that gets me. It's always been my fear that because I'm gay they'll think I'm weaker than them. Red fills my vision, and I go to push Chase again. Jabbar wraps his arms around me and holds me back, Marcus doing the same thing to Chase, who is now trying to come at me. My chest heaves in and out as I struggle to get out of Jabbar's hold. Each breath hurts, but I don't know why.

"Dude. Let me go."

This time when I jerk away, Jabbar's grip loosens. "He was joking around, Collins. What the hell?"

My head feels all foggy. I can't get my breathing under control. Holy crap, I almost just hit my best friend. Chase and I have never gotten into it. We just don't work that way.

He pulls out of Marcus's hold, breathing almost as heavily as I am. What's wrong with me? I open my mouth to tell him I'm sorry, but then his words from the other night—*it's weird*—hammer into me, mixing with what he just said. Part of me knows it was a joke, but I know the other side of it too. Chase talks crap when he's uncomfortable. I hate being the one to make him feel like that.

"Fuck you, Bradley." He shakes his head. I'm caught between being pissed and wanting to apologize.

When I don't say anything, Chase turns and walks away. Marcus and Jabbar just kind of stand there like they don't know what to do. I help make the decision for them when I go the other direction, more angry at myself than I've ever been.

MY PHONE hasn't made a sound since Friday night. Jabbar, Marcus, or Chase don't call, but why would they? I was a jerk to all of them. And it's not like TJ will call either. At least with the other guys we have thirteen years of history between us. I don't have that with TJ. He probably couldn't care less if we don't talk again.

The worst part is, I know I deserve it.

I'm sitting at the table eating a bowl of cereal when Mom comes in. It's way earlier than I'm usually up on the weekends. There's shock on her face when she sees me sitting here.

She hits power on the coffeepot, and it automatically starts brewing. "What's going on with you this weekend, Bradley?"

"Nothing."

"I'm talking to you before I have coffee. That tells you I understand how serious this is. You're my first son. I know you, sweetheart. What's wrong?"

My leg bounces up and down as I push the bowl away from me. With my elbows resting on the table, I drop my head into my hands.

"Brad." Mom moves into the chair next to me. "You're eighteen years old. You're leaving for college this summer. Let me be here for you before you don't need me anymore."

It's the sadness in her voice that does it for me. Or maybe that's an excuse, and I just don't want to admit I need her, but I tell her everything—about meeting up with TJ for the past two weeks, Chase admitting that seeing me with someone will be weird, me ending up in a fight with the guys last night, and how I walked away from TJ.

"Why is this so hard for me?" I shake my head, hating the fact that I feel like I want to cry. "I thought coming out was the hard part. I don't understand why I can't move forward, even though everyone knows."

Mom wraps an arm around me. "Oh, sweetie, of course it's hard. That's how life is. Admitting something is often only half the battle. Sometimes it's easier to admit than to follow through because that's what makes it real. It's more than just coming out—now you have to settle in."

"How?" My voice cracks.

"I don't know. I wish I did. What about TJ? Maybe it'll help to talk with him."

"Ha. Yeah, maybe if I hadn't been a jerk to him." More than once. The bulb in the kitchen flickers, and I tell myself I need to change it for Mom.

"I know these words might be foreign to you, but there's something called an apology. You could always try one of those."

I shake my head at her but also chuckle a little. "Mom's got jokes." Shrugging, I continue, "Maybe. He's leaving next week. He's doing this documentary on gay history or something for his film class."

"He's doing what?" she asks, so I explain it to her. Tell her how he has appointments set up along his path to New York. That he's talking to gay people who all have different stories and experiences. "I know there's more, but I don't remember. I—what?" I ask Mom as she stares at me with a smile on her face.

"Go with him," she says.

I pull away from her and lean back in the chair, figuring I just misheard her. "What?"

"Go with him. This is right for you, Brad. You need this. You need to step out of your bubble."

"No." I shake my head. "I can't go with him. Plus, he's going to be gone for almost two weeks, which means I'd have to miss school."

Mom pushes to her feet, excitement practically radiating off her. "You hardly ever miss, your grades are good. Basketball season is over. It wouldn't kill you to miss a few days of school."

"Um, who are you and what did you do with my mom? Aren't I supposed to be the one saying that?"

She doesn't latch on to my joke. "You're a good kid. You never get into trouble. I trust you to make the right decisions. This is important, Bradley." She kneels down in front of me. "You need to do this. I want you to see that it's okay to be who you are. This is a once in a lifetime experience for you. You need to go."

It's not until she said it that I realize how much I want to do just what she's said. The thought makes me feel... I don't know... free. "He might not want me there. And what about helping get Tyson around? And money?"

Mom stands, pushes my hair away from my forehead and kisses me there. "I'm so proud of who you are, kiddo. You talk to TJ, and I'll take care of the rest."

And I have no doubt she will.

Chapter 4

WITHOUT LETTING myself think about it, I lock myself in my room and call TJ. I look at the basketball posters on my wall as I wait, time going both too slow and too fast at the same time. He answers with a "What?" on the third ring.

"Hey." That seems to be our greeting of choice. I like the "hey" better than his "what."

"So it's cool to talk to me on the phone because your friends aren't there?" he asks.

I change positions on my bed, then do it again, not able to get comfortable. "That's not how it is." Though I'm pretty sure we both know it is. "It's not that easy for all of us." I squeeze the phone in my hand, surprised the words came out. Surprised I feel them.

TJ sighs. "It's not easy for most of us. That doesn't mean we don't try."

The line is silent for a moment, and I wonder if he hung up—if I should hang up. This was a stupid idea.

"What'd you call for, Bradley?"

"I want to go" sort of tumbles out of my mouth. The words almost echo through me, and I shove them out again, stronger this time. "I want to go."

"Go where?"

Pushing up, I sit on the edge of my bed. "On the trip, or whatever. To do your documentary. I want to help." Just saying it makes me feel like I hit the winning shot in a playoff game.

"Are you shittin' me?" TJ asks.

"No. I'm serious. I just...." Just what? I'm not sure how to finish that sentence. I just want something. Or maybe not something. Maybe I want everything.

"Not because I, like, want to hook up or anything but—"

"Because you're not really gay if you don't ever have a boyfriend?"

My fist tightens around the phone again. "That's not what I meant." It's another thing we both know I kind of did mean. "You were with that guy on Friday. I didn't know if he was, like…."

"My boyfriend?" TJ finishes for me. "We're just friends."

"Good." My heart rate goes haywire because I realize how it sounds. "Not that I care if you have a boyfriend or not. It's just—"

TJ's laugh interrupts me.

"It's not funny." Though I realize I'm smiling. I've never really had to do this, never had contact with someone who would actually be a person I'd be interested in. There have been girls, but it makes a difference if you really feel something, and I never felt any of them. Maybe it makes me a jerk for kissing them anyway. I *wanted* to feel them. I just never could.

When his laughter calms down, TJ says, "You have to admit, this came out of nowhere."

"I know. I just…."

TJ sighs but doesn't make me continue. "So we're really doing this? You're gonna drive to New York with me for the documentary?"

His questions land in my chest, swim out from there, and cement themselves into my bones. But then, what if he doesn't want me to? "I want to, if it's cool with you. I know I've been a dick. I'm sorry about the other day."

"You can definitely be a jerk."

I try to figure out what to say next but then decide to just open my mouth and speak. "I'm sorry," I say again. "If it's cool with you, I want to go… I want to go. You're the first openly gay person I've met in my whole life. I… it's lonely, ya know?" Closing my eyes, I pray he doesn't laugh. I wish I could take the words back but don't try.

It takes TJ forever to reply, but finally he does. "Yeah. I know. Let's do this."

MAYBE I really am weak because I avoid the guys the whole next week at school, and for the most part, they avoid me. Jabbar and Marcus talk to me when they're not with Chase, but since Chase and I are avoiding each other like we're allergic, that doesn't count for much.

Mom makes me invite TJ over during the week, so she can talk to him. To make things easier, I have him come when I know Chase won't be home next door. Things would be worse between us if he saw me hanging out with TJ after what went down the other night. I got in a fight with my best friend about this guy, and now I'm chillin' with him.

Mom takes a copy of his driver's license, his plate numbers, cell number, wants a copy of the route we're taking, and when we're going to be stopping in each city. TJ's cool about it and gives her everything she wants.

My leg does this crazy bouncing thing the whole time he's here. It's weird, having a guy over who isn't Chase, Marcus, or Jabbar. They're just my friends. There isn't a possibility of more with them, no questions of, do I like him, or does he like me? But with TJ there is. My stupid mind keeps wondering if Mom thinks he's my boyfriend, or that I like him, or if she thinks it would be weird to see me with him the way Chase does.

Thursday night, the day before we leave, I make my way over to Chase's house. No matter what happened, he's my boy, and I can't bail without saying something to him first—even if it is a lie.

"What's up?" I ask when he opens the front door. Chase shrugs but moves out of the way so I can go inside.

"Play a game with me," I say instead of going in.

He already has his Nikes on, so I'm not surprised when he steps right out and closes the door behind him. It's cold, but he seems to need this as much as I do. Life always feels clearer with a basketball in my hand. We play one-on-one, without much talk except curses, "nice shots," and "my ball."

When the game is over, I dribble the ball as I speak. "I was an asshole. It's just… I don't know."

Chase shrugs. "Eh. It's not like I haven't been known to be an asshole too."

I shoot the ball. Chase grabs it after it drops through the basket. "I'm bailing tomorrow. I'm gonna go stay with my uncle for a couple weeks," I tell him.

His brows draw together. "Why?"

Because I don't know how to be who I am. Admitting it isn't enough. "I have some stuff to figure out." I'm fully aware that I'm still an asshole because I'm lying to him right now.

"Cool." Chase nods. "We good?"

Words I never considered really saying to him, tease my tongue. *Stop saying things are gay. Stop telling me I'm missing out when you hook up with a girl. Don't tell me it's weird if I ever get with a guy.* None of those things leave my mouth. "Yeah, man. We're cool. Always." And we are. The truth is, if things are strange for me, I get why they are for my friends. Just like with me, they play the game, say the right things because they want them to be true. Things would be a whole lot better between all of us if we'd just admit we're all still settling in.

Chase holds his fist out for me, and I bump it with mine.

"Alright. I'm out. Thanks for the game, Collins."

He gets halfway to his house when I ask, "You riding with me to school tomorrow?"

"You kicking me out?" He grins.

"Nope."

"Then I'm there."

My feet root to the same spot until Chase gets into his house. Once he does, I grab my ball and head home.

Mom comes into my room about eleven thousand times while I'm packing. She pretends she only wants to make sure I remember this or that, but I know it's because she wants to make sure I'm doing okay. And maybe she wants to make sure she's okay too.

TJ shows up at four the next afternoon like he's supposed to.

"You have to call me every few hours, you know that right?" Mom asks.

"Yeah. You told me a million times." I grab my bags and try to hurry out the door. On reflex, I glance out the window to see if Chase is home. He's supposed to be with Jabbar but sometimes they go back to Chase's house to chill.

"I gotta go." I reach for the doorknob.

"Bradley." The tone of her voice stops me; it's firm yet soft enough that TJ can't hear her. "Are you sure you're okay with this? I don't want to push you."

I just don't want Chase to see, Mom, which maybe means I'm really not okay with this. "I want to go."

She pulls me into a hug that lasts a little too long. I see TJ freeze up when she hugs him too. A couple minutes later I'm climbing into the passenger seat of TJ's BMW X5, and we're driving away. The whole time, I'm hoping I find whatever it is I'm looking for.

Chapter 5

"NICE RIDE." I almost put my feet on the dash but figure that's not a cool thing to do in a car like this. In my car, it wouldn't matter.

"It's pretentious as hell. I hate it, but considering I didn't buy it, I didn't get a say."

"I don't know many people who'd be complaining."

TJ glances over at me as he pulls onto the freeway. "Yeah, you do. You might not realize it, but you do."

I'm pretty sure he's wrong about that, but I don't call him on it. Who would complain about a free BMW?

"You can put some music on if you want. My iPod's in the center console."

Reaching over, I pull it out and plug it in. Older rock music comes from the speakers. My head falls back against the seat as I watch the scenery go by. What do I say? Yeah, TJ and I have hung out in the past few weeks, but I don't really know him that well. Still, the music isn't enough to fill the silent space in the car, so I start drumming my thumbs on my legs as if that will help.

"It should only take us about three hours to get into Illinois. We'll probably hit traffic, so that'll make it worse. I have our hotel room reserved, and we have our first appointment tomorrow morning. I figured it would be easier to leave tonight than get up super early in the morning." He runs a hand over his spiked hair. I don't know why, but I watch the movement. He's got these string bracelets on his right wrist, in all sorts of different colors, and a black beaded one too.

"Cool. Who are we meeting with tomorrow?"

Even though he's not facing me, I see TJ roll his eyes. "Did you even look at the list?"

The way he says it makes me feel stupid. "No, not really. I thought it might be kind of cool to just go. To be surprised, ya know? Maybe that's lame." I rest my right elbow against the door of the car. My left arm jerks, then tightens when TJ reaches over and sets a hand on it. He must notice because he pulls back and sighs.

"It's not lame. I didn't expect that, though. It's neat."

"Sorry." I run a hand over my face. "I didn't mean to be weird." TJ doesn't reply, and I say "Sorry" again.

It's a few minutes later before he finally speaks. "If you wanted to be surprised, why are you asking now?"

"I don't know. I guess the silence makes me uncomfortable. It's the only thing I could think of to say." My body relaxes a little, a bit of relief settling into me at my honesty.

Tapping a finger on his chin, TJ pretends to think. "Hmm. I don't like that reason, so I'm not going to tell you."

"It's not like I can't find out."

"Yeah, but you won't." TJ smirks as though he's daring me to deny it.

"How do you know? I usually hate surprises. I piss my mom off every Christmas because I figure out what all my gifts are ahead of time."

He laughs. "First of all, you suck. That's cheating. Where's the fun in that? And second, maybe you usually hate surprises, but you never would have gone on this trip before either. You're trying to find the new you, and the new you thinks surprises kick ass."

His words strike a chord in me because they're close to home. Close, but not fully the truth. "I don't want to discover the new me. I just want to fully understand who the old one is, and to be totally okay with him."

TJ looks over and smiles. My stomach feels light when he does, but as quickly as it happens, he turns back to the road again. "We're gonna be in trouble, Bradley."

I sort of sit up a little higher in my seat. "Why? What's wrong?"

"Because I might start to like who you find." He shrugs. "And who knows if you will."

His honesty is awesome. It's cool how he just puts things out there. More people should be like that. Still, he's wrong. It's not about liking myself. I do like who I am. Contrary to my behavior lately, I'm a good guy. It's that I don't totally know how to be him yet.

That fact is proved by the way my hand automatically reaches out and turns up the music. Conversation over because I don't know how to react to knowing he might start to like me, or to the voice in my head that thinks it would be really cool if he did.

"I WANT to pay for the room," I tell TJ when we pull into the hotel parking lot. It's one of the first things I've said since our conversation a few hours before.

"Nah, don't worry about it. My parents have more money than they know what to do with. They won't even notice if they foot the bill. They wouldn't care either." TJ opens the door, but this time it's me who grabs his arm.

"Then I pay half of it. You're not paying for my stuff."

"Aww, we're going dutch. It's like a real-life first date." The playfulness in his voice makes me laugh.

"I'm serious."

"I am too. This is my trip, and they're stoked about it. They want to pay for it."

When I realize I'm still holding his arm, I jerk my hand back. "It's not fair, though. You get tonight, and I'll get the next room."

"Sure. Whatever you say." TJ gets out of the SUV and I do the same. I hang back while he checks into the room. When he's done we grab our bags and take the elevator to the third floor, room 333. I'm not sure why I pay so much attention to the room number.

Two queen beds are inside, the typical hotel flowery crap. "Why does every hotel room have to look like an eighty-year-old woman lives in it?" I drop my bag and fall onto the bed closest to the window.

"I think it's a conspiracy." TJ sets his bag on the table and immediately pulls his laptop out and hooks it up.

"What kind of conspiracy?" I ask.

"I don't know. You tell me."

I watch as he sits down and then pulls some notebooks out of his bag. I wrack my brain trying to think of something creative to say, but nothing comes. Stupid as it sounds, being in this room with him, I just realized I'm really going to be alone with a guy who isn't straight. Like sleeping in the same room for days with no parents around, alone. "I don't know."

"You say that a lot."

"Thanks for the news flash."

He shakes his head. "I didn't mean it in a bad way. Sorry. I have no filter sometimes."

I shrug because it really wasn't that big a deal. Honestly, I have no filter at times either.

With that TJ turns to face his computer and starts typing. Curiosity tugs at me. I want to go over and see what he's typing, to go through his notes and see if I can find answers to questions I don't know.

He goes back and forth between flipping through pages, and typing. He gets up for a minute to plug his camera in but then goes right back to work.

He doesn't say anything when I get up, go take a shower, and then come back out. I watch him for another minute, before asking, "You cool if I turn the TV on?"

"Go for it," he says without looking at me.

Okay.

For some reason, *SportsCenter* isn't holding my attention. I keep looking over at him, questions filling my head that don't pass my lips. Why is this so important? What does he need out of it?

The whole time I tell myself I'm not asking because he's busy and I don't want to interrupt him, but that's another lie. I'm not sure how to really be curious about these things, or how he'll feel about the fact that I am.

So instead I watch him work, see the concentration and passion in him as he does, and wonder if there's any way I'll feel the same about this by the end of the trip.

Chapter 6

TJ WAKES me up at eight the next morning. The TV's off, and all the stuff is put away. I don't even remember going to bed last night. The last thing I remember is him working, me watching TV, and now he's shaking me awake.

"We have to meet them in an hour."

Them. At least I know it's a them.

Scratching my head, I sit up. TJ's already dressed in a pair of jeans and a T-shirt that says MOVIE GUYS DO IT WITH SPECIAL EFFECTS.

"Nice shirt," I tell him. It reminds me of the first day he talked to me, and how he had his shirt on inside out. Seeing how he worked last night, I'm not surprised. He seems to be the type to get so into what he's doing that he doesn't pay attention to stuff like that.

"Made it myself."

"I never would have guessed." He moves out of the way when I stand up and walk over to my bag to grab my clothes. It takes maybe five minutes to get dressed, brush my teeth and my hair. We grab our coats and are out the door in less than another five.

"Are you hungry? We can grab something on the way or just get there early. We're meeting them at a coffeehouse, so we can always grab something there too. Catch." TJ tosses me the keys. "Can you drive? I want to make a few more notes as we go."

He's so in the zone that I'm not sure he'll even hear me when I reply to him. I climb into the driver's seat, and he gets in next to me. "Yeah, I'll drive, I can wait for food, and won't a coffeehouse be too loud?"

TJ stops fingering through his notebook and looks over at me. "Sorry, I get kind of in the zone when I'm working and I'm all over the place. They own the coffeehouse so we can use a back room. You sure about food? Oh, and here's my phone. I already put the address in for you."

I laugh but don't tell him that he's all over the place again. I also think it's sort of cool that he used the same words I did to describe him—in the zone.

He doesn't talk any more as I drive. We're a few minutes early, but TJ says he told them we might be because he'll need to set up.

After killing the engine, I lean back in my seat, letting myself focus on the tightness in my gut for the first time this morning. This is really happening. I can't believe I'm doing it. "You told them I would be here?"

He flips through pages in his notebook. "Yeah, it's no problem."

"Maybe I should hang back this first stop. I mean…." It's a whole lot easier to say I want to do something than it is to actually do it. I'm realizing now I really have to do all this stuff—talk to people and hear their stories.

He jerks his head up at that, those crazy-blue eyes like lasers looking inside me again. "What? Why would you do that?"

I shrug. "I don't know." I groan as soon as the words leave my mouth. I'm tired of not knowing.

"Brad—"

"Never mind. I'm going. Come on."

When we get inside, there are a few people our age standing behind the counter. My footsteps slow when I think they might be who we're here for, but then I remember TJ said they own the place, so I'm figuring it can't be them. The place looks pretty nice with those high tables all around and a few chairs.

"Bradley?" TJ calls. When I turn to look at him, he snaps a picture.

"What was that?"

"I'm documenting a trip, right?" He smirks.

My stomach turns over, wishing I could tell him to delete it. But then we're doing a documentary. I might have to be on camera anyway….

"TJ?" A guy walks out of a door at the end of the counter. He looks like he's about thirty-five or so. He's wearing a T-shirt with the coffeehouse logo on it. He's stacked—like seriously, so stacked I wonder how he looks like that and ever has time to leave the gym.

"Yeah, hi. It's nice to meet you." TJ holds out his hand and they shake. Then he points at me. "This is Bradley, the guy I told you about. He's helping me with the documentary. Bradley, this is Henry."

"Hey, man." I shake his hand. "Nice to meet you."

"You too." Henry leads us to another room. In the middle of it, there's a desk covered with books, papers, newspapers, and a laptop. He tells us to get set up and that he'll be back with Matt.

"Is there anything I can do?" I ask TJ when Henry leaves.

"Nah. It's okay, I got it."

So while he sets up I walk around the room and pretend there's actually a reason that I'm here. He sets up his camera on a tripod in the corner, then puts a chair on either side of it, I'm assuming for him and me. He's in his zone again, looking at the angle of the camera before positioning two other chairs. TJ looks through the camera before moving them again.

A few minutes later the door opens. Henry walks in and then... holy shit, the guy behind him is wearing eyeliner and has his nails painted. Why the hell does a guy wear eyeliner? He's like half the size of Henry, wearing a button-down shirt and a bow tie. Did I mention he's wearing eyeliner?

"Hey. I'm TJ and this is Bradley." TJ shakes Matt's hand, seemingly oblivious to the fact that he's wearing makeup.

"Nice to meet you, sweetie," Matt says, and then shakes my hand too. I manage to do it without staring at him, before I take one of the seats next to the camera.

Matt and Henry settle into the chairs opposite the ones TJ and I are in. No matter how hard I try, my eyes keep veering back to Matt. It's just something I can't comprehend. A guy like Henry, if I were older, I could be into him. TJ is hot. I love the way he spikes his hair and the blue of his eyes and... the masculinity of him. When I look at Matt, it just doesn't compute. He's a guy. Why would a guy want to look like a girl?

"Remember, if there's anything I ask that you guys don't want to answer, just tell me," TJ says to them.

"No problem," Henry replies.

"Not all the questions will be comfortable, but I really want to be as honest as I can in this."

"So should we look at you or the camera?" Matt questions.

"Us. It needs to come off naturally. Just be relaxed, like we're having a normal conversation. The red light turns blue when I'm recording." That quickly, TJ turns on the camera. When he does, Matt reaches over and sets a hand on Henry's leg.

Whoa. Maybe I'm stupid for not seeing that coming, but I didn't. They're so... different.

"How long have you two been together?" TJ asks them.

"Six years?"

"No, seven," Matt corrects Henry. "It was only a few months after I came out. I was twenty-nine."

"What about you, Henry. When did you come out?" TJ questions.

Just like TJ told them to do, they stay normal and natural talking to him as though we're not recording everything that's going on. "When I was sixteen. It wasn't on purpose, though. I was in love with my best friend. Neither of us were ready to admit it. I guess we should have been a little more careful because my mom walked in on us."

Dude... I would lose it. My face burns even thinking of something like that happening.

"What happened after that?" TJ says.

"My parents were confused more than anything. They had this stereotypical idea of what a gay man is, and I wasn't that. I could kick anyone's ass on the football field. I've always been a big guy, and they were naive. They went to his parents to try and work it out between them, but his family had other ideas. They didn't let me see him again after that. A week later they moved, and I've never seen him again."

My chest feels tight thinking of losing my best friend... of losing someone I love. And why? Because we like each other? How does that make sense?

TJ keeps going as though he's not affected by Henry's words at all. "I didn't originally plan to go this route first, but since you brought up stereotyping, I want to touch on that. The two of you are complete opposites on the surface—Henry, what some people don't consider when they think of a gay man, and Matt, maybe more so."

His statement rubs me the wrong way. Do people really think of men who wear makeup when they think of a gay guy? That's not me and never will be. The thought of being seen like that makes my skin itchy.

"We definitely get second glances when we're out in public, yes," Henry says, laughing.

"When people think of a gay couple, one of the most common misconceptions, or I guess crazy questions people ask is, who's the man in the relationship or who's the woman. Do you think you get that more because of the fact that you wear makeup, Matt?"

My head whips toward TJ. I duck, a little nervous that my shocked face will be on camera. Isn't the point of being gay the fact that there is no man and woman? Just two men, or two women?

It doesn't seem to be something Matt questions because he answers quickly. "I don't know that we get it more than other couples. It's a naive question all the way around. The point of being gay is that I'm attracted to men and so is Henry."

I'm sort of proud of the fact that I thought the same thing he said. There's so many times I'm on the outside looking in when it comes to being gay, but here, our minds ran the same track—even if it is an obvious one.

"The fact that I wear makeup doesn't make me less of a man. I just like the way it looks. I enjoy fashion and style. It doesn't mean that I want to be a woman, and it doesn't mean that I play the 'female role' in our relationship. If you want to look at it in the technical sense, in the bedroom I'm usually what a person might consider the more masculine role, which, by the way, is a bullshit way to look at it."

Did he just admit what I think he did? My eyes go wide, and I'm hoping my mouth doesn't drop open. TJ doesn't flinch, doesn't lose a shred of his concentration, and all I can do is think about what they just admitted.... Wrong or not, I'm surprised by it. The two don't seem to fit because looking at them, Henry is way more masculine than Matt.

My leg starts doing that automatic bouncing thing, and I hope no one notices. At the same time, my thumbs start drumming on my legs, my eyes now steering clear of both Henry and Matt.

"So why do you wear makeup, then?"

"Because it makes me feel good. I like the way I look. It feels right. I hid who I was for a large portion of my life. I will admit it's still hard some days. It probably doesn't make sense to someone on the outside, but the makeup makes me feel strong. It's like my armor in a way. If you would have come in here any other day, I might not even be wearing it, but I was nervous about today, and somehow, this helps."

How? I want to ask him. How can drawing attention to himself make it easier? How can that make him feel stronger?

Matt's gaze darts to the camera and then back at TJ.

"Great. Thanks for the honesty. Now I'm going to go into the reason we're here. The two of you are married, right?"

"Yes," Henry answers. "We weren't married in Illinois, though. When we got married, there were only a couple states it was legal. We actually moved for a while. Matt and I wanted to live in a place where we had equal rights to marry. It was earlier this year that we moved back." Matt glances at Henry and smiles.

"Why was that important to you? Getting married? It was obviously important enough for you to leave your home state."

The question seems like an obvious one to me. People want to get married. It's just what you do. The answer doesn't come right away, though. TJ's calm as ever and Matt and Henry are staring off into space like they forgot there's a camera on the room.

"Because our love isn't any different than the love between a heterosexual couple," Matt says. "We wanted the right to make vows to each other the way other couples are able to. Henry saved my life in a lot of ways. I'm not sure I would be here today if I hadn't met him. He taught me to be comfortable in my own skin, and he showed me that someone could love me the way I am. Don't we deserve to express our love the way heterosexual couples can?"

Matt looks at Henry, who leans over and softly kisses him. The smile Matt gives him, I think might be how Mom looked at Dad before things went to crap. He may not have loved her enough to stick around, but she always loved him. She still does. She would have given anything for Dad to return her look the way Henry does Matt's.

It makes my stomach a little queasy, but I can't help but see some similarities between myself and Matt. He didn't know how to be comfortable in his own skin, and I still don't. Not when it comes to really being gay. I never would have thought I'd have something like that in common with a guy who has eyeliner on.

TJ keeps talking to them. Asking if their relationship has changed since they got married. The answer is no, but that's not the point. They laugh and tell us about how they met and how Matt proposed to Henry, vacations they take, Henry and the gym, and their family. The longer we talk, the lighter Matt's makeup appears. Or maybe it's not that the shade changes, maybe it's me who does. I've stopped focusing on how he looks and started focusing on *him*.

As a person. Maybe it's me who realizes that despite what he wears, Matt is just like me and TJ, or hell, just like Marcus, Chase, or Jabbar.

What he wears doesn't matter. It doesn't change the person he is. We all have our form of armor; he's just a lot stronger than the rest of us because he's brave enough to let his show.

Chapter 7

"THEY WERE cool, huh?" TJ asks me as we pull back onto the freeway. We grabbed some lunch after the interview with Matt and Henry and then went back to check out of the hotel. We're going to Ohio next, and we'll be there for a couple days, he said.

"Yeah. I gotta admit, I was a little weirded out by Matt at first, though." I frown when I realize I used the same word that Chase said about me getting a boyfriend. *Weird.*

"Yeah, I had a feeling you would be. It's not a big deal, though."

TJ keeps driving while I think about what he said. "Do you ever…?"

He shakes his head. "Nope. Not my thing. I think it's brave that he does."

If someone would've told me yesterday that I'd agree with TJ about thinking of a guy wearing makeup as brave, I wouldn't have believed them. But when I open my mouth and say, "Yeah, me too," I'm being completely honest.

My friends pop into my head. What would they think if they'd seen Matt? The same as I had at first, but would they have changed how they felt by the end of the morning? Or, if I had been with them, would I let myself see Matt differently? I'm pretty sure I wouldn't like the answer.

"How long till we get to Columbus?" I ask. It's easier to concentrate on the drive rather than where we've been or where we're heading.

"Six or seven hours, depending on traffic." He pauses, in thought. "When did you realize you're gay?"

"When did *you*?"

TJ rolls his eyes. "Smooth transition, Bradley. I almost missed you avoiding the question and switching it off to me."

On reflex I punch him in the arm and chuckle. "Shut up. I'm really curious, though."

"Then why'd you tell me to shut up?"

Again I laugh. He has this corny sense of humor sometimes that I know shouldn't be funny, but it is.

"Will you tell me?" Turning, I lean against the door a little so that I can look at him.

"I don't know. Will you tell me?" TJ gives me a quick glance, letting his brows rise before paying attention to the road again. I think he's flirting. Nervous, excited electricity buzzes around inside me.

"I don't know. Maybe." I try to sound flirtatious too, but I'm not sure it's working, or if I really want it to.

He gives me that TJ headshake he does when he seems like he doesn't know what to do with me. "I think I kind of always knew. I mean, when I was young I didn't get it, but as far back as I can remember, I noticed guys. When I was about twelve, I think I really started to get it. I thought something was wrong with me, and I remember thinking that as long as no one knew, it wouldn't matter. When I was fourteen, I realized it shouldn't matter, so I came out."

I sift through the questions in my head, not sure what to ask but knowing I need to say something. "How?"

"How what?" TJ questions.

"How did you realize it shouldn't matter?" Sometimes I think you can know something, in your heart or even your head, but that doesn't change the doubt that's there. It doesn't change the hope that things could be different or that little voice that makes you feel like less than a man because of it. Do I know it shouldn't matter if I'm gay? Yep. Does that make it easier? No.

"Because it's who I am. I just don't see how being honest about who you are is a bad thing, no matter what someone else says."

For some reason, Matt pops into my head again. How he said he'd had such a hard time before meeting Henry. Before being honest and proud about who he is, even if that makes people look at him differently.

"Did you know your parents would be cool with it before you came out?"

TJ stalls, and passes a car. "Yeah. They love me. That's all that matters. I'm their son regardless."

That's something we're the same in.

"What about you? Did you know your mom would be cool with it?"

"Yeah. I'm not sure I could have come out if I didn't. That doesn't mean I wasn't freaked as well, though."

"Pfft, I'm pretty sure being scared is a prerequisite in coming out." He licks his lips, staring into the distance and looking a little lost in thought. "Why'd you come out, man?"

His question makes my muscles tense up. "What do you mean? That's a stupid question."

"No, it's not. Why'd you come out? You told your mom and your friends, but then you won't talk to me in front of them because they know I'm gay. When I asked you if you were gay at The Spot, I thought your head was going to explode or something. The hard part is over. Now you just get to *be*. Your family's cool with it, and your friends are cool with it. Not everyone's that lucky."

My hand starts to shake again, and it reminds me of how I felt when I came out to my mom—different, *less*. "Whatever."

"I'm not trying to be a jerk. I—"

"You don't think I know that?" I sit up straighter, my pulse a drum in my head. "You don't think I *get* that? Yeah, my mom is cool and the guys are cool. I'm not stupid. I hear the shit that other people have to deal with, and I know I'm lucky, but that doesn't mean I wanted this. It doesn't mean I want people to look at me funny if I'm walking down the street with a guy. It doesn't mean I want my friends to think it's weird if I get with someone. I don't want to make them uncomfortable. I did the right thing. I came out. I don't want to deal with the staring and judgment right now."

"Why does it matter that you came out if you still think there's something wrong with who you are?" There's irritation in TJ's voice, but I'm pissed too. Crossing my arms, I don't reply. He doesn't push, going silent as he drives.

Too bad I can't get his question out of my head as easily.

A SIX-HOUR car ride is a long time to be quiet. I tossed TJ fifty for gas when we stopped, and he took it. He asked what I wanted to eat when we went through a drive-thru, and I told him. Other than that we haven't really talked.

Do you want to know what else six hours is a long time for? To think. That's pretty much all I've done, the words a jumble in my head that I can't straighten out enough to make a logical sentence.

We get into Columbus at seven. As we drive, I sit up to look out the window. It's not what I expected. Who knows what I *did* expect, but this isn't it. A lot of the buildings are kind of artsy looking. I don't know if that's the right word or not. They're unique. It reminds me of TJ in some ways.

"I'll get the room," I tell him as we climb out of his vehicle.

"Okay." The first things he grabs are his laptop case and his camera bag. I'm pretty sure he could lose everything else in his life, and as long as he had those two things, he'd be good. I open my mouth to tease him, but I sort of like that about him, so I close it again.

Mom got a credit card with both our names on it when I turned eighteen, so that's what I use to pay. It's for emergencies, but she said she considered this trip one. It costs more than I thought it would, making me wonder if maybe TJ likes his pretentious car a little more than he wanted to admit. We're totally a Motel 6 kind of family.

There's no flowers in this room, which I'm stoked about, the beds covered in beige blankets. Just like last night, TJ loads up his laptop, pulls out his camera and notebooks, and gets right to work.

Shower, change, TV. Lather, rinse, repeat.

"Why does it matter that you came out if you still think there's something wrong with who you are?"

Pictures of Matt and Henry flash across the computer screen as TJ does his thing.

"What are you doing?" I ask, only to get silence.

Oh yeah. Headphones. *Awesome miss, Collins.*

Pushing off the bed, I straighten my basketball shorts, and then go over to where TJ's sitting. "Wha'cha doing?"

He pulls his headphones off, and I ask again.

"Going through some of the film frame. Then I'm going to watch the video. There's so many things I should have asked but spaced. I missed a shit-ton of opportunities on this one."

"Really? I was wondering the whole time how you knew to ask things I never would have thought about." And it's true. Some of the questions he had written out, but a lot he thought of on the fly. "What's film frame?"

TJ looks up at me. I wonder how stiff the spikes in his hair feel.

"Still images used to make a moving picture. Do you wanna watch it with me?"

"Yeah." I shrug. "Sure."

He grabs a chair and pulls it over. When I sit down next to him, our legs touch, his jeans against my shorts and my skin. That stupid voice in my head tells me to pull back, but this time I ignore it.

TJ unplugs the headphones, and as Matt and Henry's voices fill the room, I let mine rise over theirs. "Thanks. For letting me come, or whatever. I'm glad I'm here." Translation: I'm also sorry for being a dickhead today.

TJ nudges my arm with his. "I'm glad you're here too."

I'm caught between just wanting his words to be 100 percent true, and also hoping they translate into *it's okay.*

Chapter 8

TJ COMES out of the bathroom without his shirt on the next morning.
I'm around guys in the locker room all the time and have played basketball shirtless more times than I can count, but I've never had my eyes drawn to another guy in those instances. It's different with my friends because they're just that, friends. Plus, they're into girls. I know it and they know it and my body gets it too. I don't see them that way because the possibility isn't there, but there's possibility with TJ... and I'm seeing him.

Seeing the difference in his black hair when it's flat against his head and not spiked at the top. Seeing the contours of his muscles and the way they move and yeah... he might be a film guy, but he's hot too.

His body matches mine in every way, but at the same time, it's like I've never seen a male body before. I guess because I've never seen *him.*

TJ lifts his arms and pulls a camo shirt over his head. When he does, his eyes meet mine. Automatically I whip my head in the other direction, pissed at myself for breaking eye contact. I'm an eighteen-year-old guy, and I've never kissed a person I really wanted to. I definitely shouldn't be embarrassed about checking someone out. Chase, Jabbar, and Marcus haven't held in their ogling stares since we were fourteen. Chase lost his virginity our freshman year.

I hear soft footsteps on carpet as TJ moves closer to me. The bed dips when he sits down, and my heart starts going crazy.

TJ's hand cups my cheek. There's a little callus on his finger, probably from the pencil since he writes in his notebook so much.

"There's nothing wrong with who we are." His voice is softer than I've ever heard it. I cock my head back because it surprises me, but then he's leaning forward. *Finally.* No eighteen-year-old guy should be without his first kiss, but I can't count the girls. It doesn't feel right.

Coming out didn't prepare me for this because words and actions are two totally different things, but I want it and don't at the same time.

Because this makes it real. This makes it more than words, and even more than before I see that words are cake compared to actions.

But also, *finally, finally, finally,* I'm going to kiss a guy. His lips are close to mine. I think about the fact that I didn't shave this morning and wonder if he'll like it and right before we touch... *ring!*

I jerk back as my cell phone goes off again. TJ laughs because it's obviously the funniest thing in the world since he's already done this. He's had *this.* That thing that I've done with girls because it's what guys do, but have never been lucky enough to really *feel* it.

"What?" I say into the phone as Mom says, "Well, good morning to you too."

TJ's still laughing, so I grab a pillow off the bed and throw it at him, hoping he realizes I'm going to kick his ass later. But I'm smiling too. Yeah... I'm totally smiling.

TJ HAS me drive again while he writes and reads through his notebook. He stuck with the plan of not telling me where we're going, even though I've asked him a couple times. Anytime I say something, I'm not sure if he's really even listening to me or not. He just mumbles an answer and then starts scribbling again.

Watching him be completely into what he's doing makes me feel like I'm seeing something private, something that's such a part of who he is that he must trust me to let me see it. Then I realize that sounds ridiculous, and I wonder if he slipped something into my water to make me overthink everything.

"This looks like an abandoned building." I check out the boarded-up windows, while letting the SUV idle off the side of the road. "Are you sure this is the right address?"

"Yeah. We also can't record his face, or use his name." TJ looks at me. "He was nervous about you. I promised him you were cool, though."

Drum, drum, drum. My thumbs slap down on my thighs over and over. "Yeah, it's cool. Who is he?" It's obvious whoever he is, he isn't out.

"You'll see. Just don't act surprised. Come on." He nods toward the building and then gets out. I follow behind him, carrying the laptop bag while TJ carries the camera. The air isn't as cool as it could be, with the sun out and just a crisp breeze around us.

"We have to go around back, he said." TJ heads around the left of the building and goes to the back where there's not a street. My mind wanders, and I wonder what kind of building it was before it shut down—some kind of factory, I'm guessing.

We crawl through one of the broken windows. With each step we take, I'm expecting the Secret Service or something to jump out from hiding somewhere—armed guards or some shit with all this secrecy. Either that, or we're about to accidentally walk in on a drug deal and get shot.

TJ leads the way to a back corner. There are huge windows about thirty feet up the wall that aren't boarded up, making it bright enough to see. The second we get close, I know exactly why this is going down the way it is. Standing in front of us is the center for one of the best college basketball teams in the nation.

"Hey." He nods but sort of looks down like that will keep us from recognizing him.

My mouth opens, and the words "It's okay. I play ball too." just sort of fall out.

He looks up at me, rubs a hand over the dark skin of his other arm. "What's up?"

I told my hand out to him. "I'm Bradley. This is TJ. Yeah, that was stupid. You already know who he is." I just want to keep talking to hopefully make him more comfortable, though.

We shake, and then he does the same with TJ, who says, "We'll get set up real quick." As we step away, he squeezes my shoulder, and I nod.

TJ puts the camera on the tripod. "What do you want us to call you?" he asks.

"I don't know.... Dustin?"

We both nod. There are old chairs in the building already, making me wonder if this is a place he comes to get away or something. But then I remember he doesn't even go to school here... maybe this is where he's from.

The camera is turned so only TJ and I will be in view. We sit down, but Dustin doesn't, pacing back and forth.

"Let me know when you're ready," TJ tells him calmly. He's good at this.

TJ explains to him just to act natural and talk. It's different because we're not actually recording Dustin the way we did Matt and

Henry, but I think TJ's trying to relax him by speaking too. After a few minutes, Dustin nods, and TJ turns the camera on with the remote.

Like I did with Matt and Henry, I sort of hang out on the sidelines.

"Hi, Dustin. Thanks for speaking with us today."

He clears his throat. "No problem."

"Do you want to talk about why you aren't on camera?" TJ questions.

"Because I'm not out, obviously."

"Do you feel like coming out is something you can't do?"

"That's a stupid question. Shit. Sorry. I can't. I know it's something I can't do."

TJ nods. "Can you tell us a little about your family? How you were raised."

Dustin keeps pacing, pacing and not talking. It goes on so long I start moving around in my seat, uncomfortable.

"If you don't want to talk about that, we don't have to," TJ tells him.

"No." He sighs. "No, we can. It's just... I was raised Baptist. It was all I ever knew growing up, Sundays, Bible study. I can quote almost any Scripture you ask. And I believe. I do. I mean, how could we have gotten here, if there isn't a higher power?" Dustin asks, conviction in his voice. It gives me the chills, not because I agree with him or don't but because I hear the pain in his voice. It cracks when he speaks. He talks more softly than he should. I hear how much this tears him apart.

"When I was a kid," Dustin starts again. "I heard my parents talkin'. Shit." He shakes his head. "I don't know if I should tell this story."

"We can edit it, right, TJ?" I ask him. "I mean, if you want. You can tell us, and then TJ can edit it out." I'm not sure if I can tell that Dustin really wants to tell this story or if I just really need to hear it. Maybe both.

TJ nods. "Yeah, we can take it out. Like we talked about, I won't put anything in you don't want me to."

It's then I realize how much TJ and Dustin have probably spoken before. That TJ might know all this, and they must have formed some kind of relationship for Dustin to trust him.

For the first time since this started, Dustin stops moving. He kneels down, puts his elbows on his knees and his head in his hands.

"When I was thirteen years old I heard my parents talking with someone from our church. The other people were cryin', cryin' so hard I thought someone died—to them, they had. Their daughter told them she was a lesbian and introduced them to her girlfriend. They'd met at college and they were in love, she told them.

"But they couldn't...." Dustin shakes his head. "They couldn't handle it. They told her if she wouldn't be straight, if she wouldn't do *right*, then they didn't want nothin' to do with her. That she wouldn't be their child anymore."

Dustin rocks back and forth. There's a weight in my gut getting heavier and heavier by the second. The urge to hug him washes over me. I've never hugged a guy I didn't know in my whole life.

"I waited... waited for my parents to tell them they were wrong. She was their kid and they should love her no matter what. Do you know what they said?" he asks.

"What?" I'm glad TJ answers because I can't find my voice.

"They told the couple they were right. That she went against God, and the whole time I'm shaking. Shaking because that meant those things I was feelin' meant I was goin' against God too. That I was wrong. And I knew if I told my parents, I'd be dead to them too."

The building is completely quiet. My head is foggy, like I'm trying to work my way through this maze that I can't see.

"Have you ever told anyone?" TJ asks him. "Have you told anyone except us?"

My gaze finds TJ, and I wonder how he can still form questions right now. My eyes drift back to Dustin. The guy is a monster on the court, no one fucks with him, but right now he's bent over and rocking. He looks broken. Broken and alone. Scared.

He shrugs. "Anonymous stuff online, like where we met. Do you know how it feels for no one in your life to know who you are? To lie to everyone so much that you start to believe it? Then you see a guy you like or have to screw around with a girl so no one wonders." He shakes his head, rubs his face. "I feel alone... like there's no one in the world like me. I'm different and I go against God."

"No you don't," I tell him. The words are like a battering ram, breaking through my lips. They need to come out, and I need Dustin to believe them. Need to believe them myself. "No you don't. And you're not alone."

Chapter 9

DUSTIN GOES on to talk about sports, and his fears of coming out, not just because of his family but because of who he is.

"I'm thinking about proposing to my girlfriend. I mean, she's great. I really do love her. I'm just not in love with her. Maybe I can be, though. If I try hard enough, maybe I can make it happen."

I open my mouth to tell him no, that it's not fair to him or to her, but TJ speaks first. "Would it work? Falling in love with her, I mean."

Dustin shakes his head. "I won't really do it. Can't. She doesn't deserve that."

"So what will you do?" I ask him.

He looks at me, but it's almost like he's seeing through me. Like he's already checked out. "Keep pretending."

None of us talk much as the interview finishes up. My whole body is dead weight, almost too much for me to carry. Dustin walks around with his hands deep in his pockets and his head down. It's as though the room is as heavy as my body, thick and uncomfortable.

Stepping up beside TJ, I lean close to him. "We're going to be here a couple days, right?"

He pushes his camera into the bag. "Yeah."

"Maybe we can see if he wants to hang out? We can go do something or he can go back to the hotel with us. I just... I feel really bad." I've never experienced being that alone. I've always had someone.

TJ sort of studies me. He cocks his head, and I start feeling under the microscope. I shift my weight from one foot to the other, one question playing on repeat. *What does he see?*

"Yeah, sure. That'd be fine." He's still looking at me weird, making me rub my hand over my face to make sure I don't have something on it. TJ smiles like he knows what I'm doing. My stomach gets light. He has a dimple under the right side of his mouth that I've never noticed before. Out of nowhere this crazy curiosity fills me up, and I question if he sees something like that on me. If he ever noticed the gold Mom always talks about in my brown eyes, or the way my hair falls on my forehead, or if he can read my mind and realize I'm turning into a sap.

"Are you going to go ask him?" TJ grins.

Duh. "Oh yeah. Definitely. I'll be back."

Dustin looks up at me when I approach and rubs a hand over his shaved head. I think about calling him by his real name, but I don't know if I should. He said to call him Dustin. Maybe that somehow makes it easier for him to pretend he's someone different. Before I get a chance to call him anything, he says, "You guys can do that voice thing, right? So no one can recognize how I sound."

I have no idea. "I'll talk to TJ. We'll find a way, and if it doesn't work, we won't put you in the documentary if you don't want. You can trust him."

He nods. "Are you out? That was a dumb question. You just had your face on the camera."

"No, it wasn't a dumb question, but yeah... I am."

"Your parents were cool with it?"

"My mom was. She said she already knew. My dad bailed a long time ago, though."

Kicking at something on the ground, he continues, "He your boyfriend?"

He doesn't look me in the eyes as he speaks. One word rolls off his body language... *alone, alone, alone.*

"No. I've never had a boyfriend. Never been with a guy at all." I shrug. "I guess I'm kind of afraid."

At that Dustin's eyes jerk to me. "But you're out. Your mom's cool with it. What do you have to be afraid of?"

My stock answer is the only one I have. "I don't know. Listen, we were thinking about finding something fun to do tonight—or even staying in the hotel room and ordering pizza or something. You wanna hang with us? You can—"

"Nah. I can't. I need to... I just can't."

It's there inside me, the need to push, but I don't give in to it. He's trying as much as he can. "Okay. If you ever want to talk, TJ knows how to get ahold of me. I mean, it's not like I really have it together, but yeah, I'm here."

He reaches out to shake my hand. "Thanks, man."

"No problem, Dustin."

"You… you know who I am, right?"

I nod.

"You can call me by my real name. Not in the documentary or anything, but here."

This moment is important, though I'm not sure exactly why. "Thanks for everything, Shaun."

"It feels good, someone who knows calling me by my name. You guys are the only people who know me." Shaun doesn't say another word. He doesn't talk to TJ. He just turns, walks away, climbs through the same window we did, and he's gone.

THE SILENCE on the way back to the hotel is different than any other silence I've shared with TJ. There's something to be said for silence, I think. There's a lot you can discover about a person in the quiet moments, a lot you can discover by which moments they choose for silence, or by watching their body language during it.

TJ's body is slumped. He licks his lips every few minutes. He starts to bite his nails. I've never seen him bite his nails before.

He seems almost as broken as Shaun was when he left. TJ doesn't get broken. He's the guy who comes out, and has boyfriends, and makes documentaries. If he likes a guy, he approaches them without worrying about what anyone else thinks.

All of our silences before have come from me being a jerk, but this one is just as much TJ as it is me. Maybe more so.

"Are you okay?" I ask him.

"No. I'm fucking pissed is what I am. I mean, what's wrong with that guy? What's so wrong with Shaun that he has to lie about who he is? Why does he have to pretend to be someone else so his family will love him? That's not love, Bradley, that's…. Ugh! I don't even know what that is!"

He jerks the car to the right. Another one honks at us, but TJ ignores it, continuing to cut them off, and then pulls off into a parking lot. As soon as he has the car parked, his hands slam down on the steering wheel over and over, pain and anger echoing into the vehicle with each hit.

"Hey." I grab the arm closest to me.

TJ tries to jerk free, but I don't let him. Instead he turns to me, blue fire in his eyes. "What's wrong with him? I mean, you're embarrassed to be who you are too, so why don't you tell me? What are you afraid people will think about you?"

Ice crystalizes every inch of me, anger and guilt freezing it further. This time when he pulls his arm, my fingers open up. The only sounds in the car are his heavy breaths mixing with mine.

For the first time, it's TJ who shoves open the door. TJ who angrily pushes out of the car. TJ who makes the vehicle rattle when he slams the door. TJ who always has it together, who leans against the car. TJ, the mecca of all things gay, who runs his hands through his hair and drops his head. TJ who is lost.

My movements are in slow motion as I open the door. Get out. Close the door. Walk over to him. My heart beats in slow motion too.

"Shit." He drops his arms to his sides. "I'm sorry. I didn't mean to say that. I don't get it, though. He's a good guy. That's all that should matter. I don't get why his own parents wouldn't want him if they knew."

"I don't know."

Humorlessly, he chuckles. "That's the first time I agree with you on that answer."

I can't return the laugh, so instead I lean against the SUV next to him. It takes me a few minutes to find the words I'm looking for, but when I do, they kind of pour out of me. "I didn't get it before. I've never known what it felt like to be alone like that. I always knew I'd have my mom. I worried about the guys a little, but we've been best friends our whole life, so I couldn't really even imagine my life without them in it. I've never known what it felt like to be alone," I say again.

TJ waits for me to continue.

"Mom's been on my back ever since I came out about talking with other gay kids, or meeting other gay kids, people, adults, whoever, and it used to piss me off so much. Why did I have to search for other gay people? Why should it matter if I knew anyone else who is gay or not? And in some ways, maybe it doesn't. People are people, but I look at him. At Shaun, who feels so alone.... Like no one knows him. He wants to be around people who he feels are like him. When I see that, I kind of get it, because even if I didn't think I needed it, maybe someone else does. Maybe I could have saved someone from feeling alone."

Or maybe I'd finally admit there's a part of me who feels a little alone too.

Chapter 10

TJ STEPS away from the SUV and looks at me. "You were awesome today. With Matt and Henry I could tell you wanted to fade into the background, but you weren't like that today. Even from the beginning when you told him you're into sports, up until asking him to hang out with us. It might not seem like a lot, but it was something."

"Didn't feel like it. It was the right thing to do."

TJ shrugs. "Most people don't try to do the right thing. Maybe if we did, this whole thing wouldn't be so hard."

Yeah, only it's not hard for him.

TJ nudges me. "I don't want to go sit in our hotel room all day. It feels wrong. Depressing. Wanna go grab some food or something?"

"Yeah, sure." I shrug and go to walk around the car, but TJ reaches out and grabs my wrist. The warmth of his skin makes my temperature kick up a notch. My eyes almost dart down to see where he's touching me, but I fight it.

"I shouldn't have said what I did. It's just... I don't get how parents can be like that, and I hate it. I shouldn't have taken it out on you."

But he wasn't really that far off in his assessment. There are times I'm embarrassed of who I am. "Come on. Let's go get some food. I'm freaking starving."

We jump into his SUV, and then TJ pulls out onto the road again. "What kind of food do you like?" he asks.

"The kind you eat. That's pretty much my only stipulation. Food is food. Here"—I pull my cell out of my pocket—"I'll look up some places and see what I can find."

It takes a couple minutes, but then I tell him, "There's a place called Easton Town Center and then another called Short North. Short North doesn't seem as big. It's got food, but it looks like it has a lot of art galleries and crap like that too."

TJ gets a smile that's, like, as big as my head.

"I take it that's a good thing?" I ask him.

"Dude, I love art, anything creative, really. It's awesome to see things that come from someone else's imagination. You don't like galleries?"

"Umm…." I scratch my forehead so my hand is blocking part of my face. "I haven't really been to one."

TJ shakes his head and lets out a deep breath, but there's still a smile tugging at his lips. "What is with you sports guys? We're totally going there. Tell me you want to go… what's it? South North? What kind of name is that?"

I'm not sure if he's joking or not, but I still chuckle. "Short North, art guy. Yeah, sure. I wanna go there."

"Then *come on*." He reaches for my phone, but I pull it back. "Do your job. I'm the driver, you're the navigator. Navigate."

"I'm doing it. Damn. When did you get so pushy?" Not that I don't think TJ could always be pushy, only it's not really in a bad way. He's passionate about things, and it's contagious. I've never given a second thought to an art gallery in my life, but my fingers are suddenly moving too fast to type the right letters, and I'm wondering what it is that he sees to make him so excited.

Finally I get the address in, and my phone starts giving us directions.

We get there and park. I swear TJ almost has a skip or something in his step as he starts to head toward the outdoor art district.

"We're eating first."

He looks back at me. "We're not eating first."

"My stomach is growling, man. Maybe you aren't eating first, but I am."

He stops and waits for me to catch up to him. When I get to him, his stomach grumbles too. "Yeah, okay, let's eat first."

We both laugh as we start walking again. We end up eating at a Cajun food place. I've never had Cajun before. The rice and meat burns my mouth like crazy, but it's good.

"You like it?" he asks me.

"Yep. You?" I take another bite of my jambalaya.

"Yeah. We eat a ton of different stuff. My parents are food snobs. I think they really do believe you are what you eat, so most of the time it's shit that costs way more than any meal should. I think when I leave for college, I'm going to eat nothing but fast food. At least for a few months or something. I'm more of a fast food kind of guy."

"Really?" Leaning back in my chair, I cross my arms. "I didn't get that impression when you've talked about your parents before."

TJ's lips stretch into a thin line. "I go to Brice Private School, remember?"

I drop my head back and laugh. "Oh yeah. I forget you're a private school rich kid. You don't seem like it."

"And I forget you're a sports guy too. Not that I really have anything against sports. I think it's only in high school that the prerequisite is being an asshole."

"Hey."

TJ shrugs. "Except you, I guess."

I don't know why, but I smile at that. "Yeah? I thought you'd think I was an asshole. I've been one to you a lot."

He gets a little grin. "We all have our moments. Yours are getting a little further between, though."

The waiter comes up and asks us if we want anything else. Both of us say no, and then he sets a check on the table. "How much is it? We can half it."

"I got it."

He obviously has money, and it's cool that his parents are so supportive about this trip that they don't mind what he spends. Still it doesn't feel right to have him buy my stuff. "No, you shouldn't have to pay for my food. We're splitting rooms and gas. We should do it for food too."

"No one said I was doing it because I have to." He pauses a second and says, "I want to buy you lunch."

It feels like a totally girly thing to do, but I start wondering if this is like a date or something. I mean, lunch is a date thing, and TJ wants to buy, and holy shit, I might be on my first date with another guy.

The question is, do I want to be on a date with TJ?

When I look at him, I notice that dimple again and see the light dusting of hair because he must have been too excited to shave this morning. I think about how he looks when he gets into his zone with this documentary, which makes him forget about everything going on around him. The fact that he's doing the documentary at all, when something like that never would have even occurred to me, and if it had, I probably wouldn't have had the balls to follow through alone.

And yeah, I totally want to be on a date with him right now, but I also want to stop overthinking it.

"Cool. I want to buy you dinner, though."

"Yes," he says, easy as that, before pulling his wallet out of his back pocket and setting the credit card down.

After the waiter takes our payment, we head out of the restaurant and in search of TJ's art galleries.

"I can't believe I never knew this place existed. Look at this." TJ points to a sign. "They have a gallery hop the first Saturday of every month."

"Awesome," I tell him because I'm not sure what else to say.

"You have issues. You're not into this at all, are you?"

He overexaggerates his stumble when I playfully push him. "I don't have issues. And it's not that I'm not into it, it's just...." I grin. "I'm totally not into it. But that's okay. We can still check it out."

TJ shakes his head. "Come on, sports guy. I'm making it my personal mission to change your view on a lot of things before this trip is over." He grabs my shirt and starts pulling me along. I go easily, but TJ doesn't let go of my clothes. My eyes automatically jerk to the left, then the right, to see if anyone is looking at us strangely.

It's wrong and I can't help it. Or maybe I can. Either way, TJ lets go when we head into the first gallery, and I release a relieved breath. Crazy how just a few minutes ago I realized I wanted to be on a date with him, and now I'm already right back to stressing about how people will look at me if I am.

Chapter 11

MOST EVERYTHING the first gallery is showing are flowers and rivers and forests. I definitely don't get the draw here, and though TJ takes the time to look at everything, we don't stay long.

It's the second gallery where TJ perks up a little. He heads straight back to this one section where all the pictures are full of different colors and designs that look like something I'd paint. Or a ten-year-old.

"What is this?" I ask him, pointing to one.

"I don't know."

My nose wrinkles. "Okay."

"These are abstract. Who really knows what some of them are or what they mean. It's probably something different to everyone. That's what makes them so incredible."

"How do you mean?" We continue walking through the gallery. There's a little shock inside me because I really am interested in what he's saying.

"I don't know. It's personal. Most things in this world are. We're all going to take a situation and pull something different out of it. It just depends on who you are. Take being gay for example—see, you flinched when I said the word."

"No I didn't." But I probably did.

"Whatever. The point is, you're gay, you know you're gay, everyone in your life knows you're gay. You came out young, which a lot of people don't have the guts to do, but you're still freaked out by it. That's something personal in you. The question is why? And if you're so uncomfortable about it, why did you come out in the first place?"

What the hell is he talking about? We were talking about art, and now he's dissecting me. "Because it was the right thing to do. I didn't want to lie to everyone in my life. I'm stronger than that."

TJ pauses for a second. The corners of his eyes wrinkle as he looks at me. "Maybe it was the right thing for you to do, but look at Shaun. Maybe it's not the right thing for him, at least not right now.

That's where your personal experience comes in. What makes me curious is why it was so important for you to come out, but if I reached over and grabbed your hand right now, you'd probably lose it."

At that I stop walking.... But I'm curious too. I want to know why just like he does. Why is it so hard for me to show the person I really am? The person everyone knows is inside me? It's something personal, like he said. I see something different in my abstract life than he does.

"Has it always been easy for you?" I ask him.

"Nothing's easy all the time, Bradley. Whether it's hard or not doesn't change the facts. I'm gay. I always will be. And so will you. I'm okay with that, and the people who aren't okay with it can kiss my ass."

TJ's eyes look dull for the first time. There's a sadness there he doesn't usually carry—or doesn't usually show, I guess. As quickly as it comes, he wipes it away. "Anyway, if you can capture that personal, crazy feel of emotions in art, it's amazing." He nods. "Come on, sports guy, I'm not done with you."

I try to smile at him, but my mind is still mulling over what he said. "Lead the way, film boy."

It's the third gallery we go into that TJ goes all *in the zone* at. One painting really. He stands in front of this one particular painting, looking at the art in a way I'm not sure I've ever looked at anything in my life. I suddenly wish I had.

Studying it, I try to see what he does. Try to figure out what makes it so special or what it could mean. The clouds look like arms reaching toward the ground, the rain like tears falling down. There are hills and trees on the ground that look as though they're reaching for the sky too.

"What is it?" I ask him.

"I took a class on creation myths, from different cultures last year. This is the Maori creation myth. Do you know it?"

I raise a brow and TJ laughs. "I didn't want to assume. Just thought I'd ask." He pauses for a minute before he continues. "That class was actually harder than it sounds, so I don't remember all the names and stuff—"

"I'm glad my school doesn't offer it. I already thought it sounded hard."

He nudges my arm. "Whatever. Anyway, as I was saying. The story, it starts out with two people in love."

"Don't they always."

"Stop interrupting."

Like happens so often when I'm around him, I laugh.

"Anyway, two people or beings or whatever are in love with each other. They're so in love that they're always holding each other tightly. They have all sorts of kids, I don't remember all their names, but they're each gods of something like water, or air. The only one I remember is Tane because I thought that was a badass name. He was the god of the forest. So yeah, these two, like, infinite beings were in love, were always holding each other, and their kids were forced to live between them.

"As you can assume the kids didn't like that very much. They decided to use all their strength to force their parents apart, who became—"

"The sky and the ground," I finish for him. Now, the way the clouds reach toward the land, and the way the land tries to reach the sky, makes sense.

"Yeah. It's like The Earth Mother and the Sky Father or something. I might be getting them mixed up. They say when it rains, the sky is crying for their lost love, the same for the Earth when mist drifts up for the sky."

This feeling of sadness drapes over me when I look at the painting this time.

"I know it's crazy, and the myth very distinctly says 'he and she,' but I always kind of thought of it in the same way as being gay— people who love each other being forced apart because of what someone else wants, or what makes them more comfortable."

It's in this moment that I get it. I get TJ's fascination with creating and how we each bring our personal experience to something like art. Because ever since he told the story, I can't help but think about how it would feel to get pushed away from someone I love the way they were in the myth.

"DUDE, LOOK at that." I point to a sign in front of us that says Out of the Closet Thrift Store. A secondhand store has never really grabbed my attention before, but with the name, my interest is automatically piqued. "Have you heard of it?" I ask TJ.

"No. Come on. Let's go check it out."

"Whoa. You're like the master of all things. I can't believe you don't know what it is," I tease and TJ frowns.

"What do you mean?"

"I mean you have all the answers. You have everything figured out." I shrug and then start feeling like an idiot. "Never mind." I turn away.

"Yeah. I am pretty good, huh?" TJ teases.

"Whatever. I take that back." TJ stumbles when I push him, but he somehow grabs my arm, and I almost trip too. We're both laughing when we walk through the door of the thrift store. It's huge, and unlike any thrift store I've ever seen, which admittedly isn't a lot.

"Hi. Can I help you?" A girl with a thousand braids in her hair walks up to us.

"We've never heard of this place before. What is it?" TJ says. "I mean, obviously a thrift store but—"

The girl interrupts before TJ can finish, telling us all about Out of the Closet. She goes on and on about how they benefit the AIDS foundation. Some locations actually do AIDS testing and all sorts of other stuff. TJ's obviously in TJ-Land; his eyes all wide and excited as he asks her a million questions.

It makes me an asshole, I'm fully aware of that, but I just keep hearing the word, AIDS, AIDS, AIDS, over and over. That's some scary shit.

I'm not an idiot. I know you can't catch AIDS from talking to someone who has it, or from being around them, but the truth is, I've never known someone who is positive. It's been hammered into my head over and over how bad it is, and there's this stigma around it that makes me suddenly uncomfortable.

Is she positive? As soon as the question pops into my head, I groan, pissed at myself for wondering it. Who cares if she is?

Sort of standing back, I let TJ do his thing. He hasn't stopped with the questions since she started answering them, and now he's finding out all sorts of information about donating and other locations and blah, blah, blah. It's so freaking cool of him. I get that, and the longer I stand here watching, I wonder why it's so easy for him to be who he is. Why it's so easy for him to just accept anyone and everyone, and wishing I was a little more like that.

By the time we leave the store, half of me is thinking *finally* and the other part is calling myself the douchebag I know I'm being.

When we get back to the hotel, neither of us really feel like going out. We grab chips and a bunch of junk food from a store next door, and then head back to our room.

TJ's sitting in front of his computer screwing around with his video, while I'm chillin' on my bed when he turns around and says, "Hey."

"Yeah?" I reply.

"The thrift store was an awesome find. Today was a cool day."

"It was a cool day." I nod at him, wondering if he means it was a good day because of the store or because of hanging out with me.

Chapter 12

LIKE THE other two times, I drive to our appointment the next day. TJ's doing his thing in the passenger seat. Every now and again, I find myself glancing over at him.

"You're watching me, sports guy."

"Maybe you're interesting, film boy."

He turns his head a little, still leaning forward, and gives me a half smile. "You think I'm interesting. I can work with that." Then his eyes look down again, studying the papers in his lap.

Me? I'm wondering what he means. There are a million ways a guy can take that. "You can work with that? Like how?"

"Shh. I'm busy, Bradley. We have an appointment in less than fifteen minutes."

His cheek pulls back, telling me he's smiling.

"Exactly, in fifteen minutes. Take it from me, procrastination is key. Oh, hey. I just rhymed."

TJ falls backward, head against the seat, and laughs. "You did not just say that."

"What? You make movies and love art, I spit sick rhymes." I like the sound of his laugh and like knowing I'm the one making him do it. Believe me, if that wasn't the case, the words *spit sick rhymes* never would have come out of my mouth. "Don't be jealous of my talent. Just remember, one day you'll be able to say you knew me."

He shakes his head. "I'm not sure if I want anyone to find out I know you and that's not what I was talking about. I would never doubt your mad rapping skills. I just can't believe someone could ever say the words *procrastination is key*, in regards to something as kick-ass as what I'm doing. You know who I am, right?"

Chuckling, I make a right turn. "I do."

"And one day you'll be able to say you knew me. People will be like—no way! You knew TJ Bennett? What was he like? Was he cute? I can't believe you made a documentary with him."

For some reason, I don't doubt that he's right. And I also suddenly want to know more about him. "Do you only wanna make documentaries and stuff like that, or do you want to make movies too?" It feels strange to me that this conversation hasn't come up before. What he does is obviously such a huge part of who TJ is.

"Movies. I want to entertain people—to make them laugh or cry. To make them happy or sad but also to... I don't know, make them think. I can do both, I think. Entertain and open people's eyes. Too many people walk around with them closed."

A deep breath pushes out of my lungs. TJ must notice because he says, "I didn't mean you."

"But that doesn't make it any less true."

I tense up a little when TJ reaches over and touches my leg. I wish I could take it back, but he's already starting to pull away, so I do the only thing I can think of. I reach over, grab it, and put it back. Needing to feel, to know who it is, and see that it's okay. The way he touches me is okay, and it's the way I want to be touched by him.

TJ doesn't move, and I start to wonder if he's keeping his hand there just because I want it. But then his thumb brushes my thigh. I squeeze the steering wheel determined not to make us wreck from that hurricane of different emotions inside me.

When the phone tells us we've reached our destination, I pull over, turn off the car, and stare at the hand on my lap. My hands shake as I draw each of his fingers with the tip of mine, up his pinky, back down. Up his ring finger and back down that again. It's warm and soft, and maybe the same size as mine.

"I don't want to live with my eyes closed, TJ." Those words never would have come out of my mouth with anyone else.

"You won't." TJ makes me want to believe him.

He pulls his hand back, and my skin starts to go hot. I'm not sure if it's all embarrassment or if there's want mixed in. The second TJ grabs his notebooks, he's in his zone again. Shaking my head, I try to join him there. Try not to concentrate on the fact that for the first time in my life, I'm really into someone.

We grab all the stuff out of the SUV before heading toward the small, brick house with a rainbow flag painted on the door. "Who lives here?" I ask as we walk down the cracked sidewalk. The air is warmer today than it was yesterday but still chilly.

"The guy we're going to see." He grins but then stumbles over a broken piece of pavement and almost falls.

"That's what you get for being sarcastic. I mean who are we seeing today?"

"Well, I kind of lied anyway. It's the boyfriend of the guy we're seeing. They both go to college here, but Dave lives off campus, Richie lives on campus. It's Richie who I've been talking to. That's all I'm going to tell you."

I'm totally regretting my plan to be surprised by each of our stops. TJ doesn't give me a chance to try and talk him out of it before he knocks on the door. "You suck." As soon as the words leave my mouth the door opens and then... well then I'm struck stupid. Richie, Dave, whoever the heck the guy is, is freaking hot. The slightly warmer air I was just thinking about has nothing on the heat frying my insides right now.

He's got blond, kind of messy hair. He's wearing what looks like a basketball jersey with the name of his college on it and no shirt beneath it. There's no number on the jersey and the material isn't the same, so I know it's not real but, dude, why am I worrying about his shirt anyway? He's probably the hottest guy I've ever seen in real life.

"TJ? Hey, man. What's up?" He says before he leans in and hugs him. At that I pull back a little, not sure if it's because I don't like him hugging TJ, or I'm jealous that TJ gets to touch him.

"Hey. Nice to meet you. This is Bradley, the guy I told you about." TJ points over his shoulder to me. "Brad, this is Richie."

Richie looks in my direction and smiles. He holds out his hand, but mine won't fucking move. My brain is shooting on all cylinders, and the whole time I know I should be moving or saying something, but all I can think about is this very real, hot gay guy is talking to me. I mean, TJ is good-looking, there's no doubt about it but—"Bradley."

I let my eyes dart to TJ when he speaks and notice his brows are pulled together. A second later the look slides off his face, and I'm able to mumble, "Hey. Nice to meet you," to Richie while looking at the ground.

Real awesome, right?

"Come on in." Richie steps inside and walks, expecting us to follow him. Before I can go inside I feel TJ's hand on my arm.

"Need to adjust your pants or something?"

My hand flies down and so do my eyes. As soon as they do, TJ laughs. "If you had to look, that means it was possible something was showing."

Jerk. "Fuck off. I don't have a boner."

"Did someone say boner?" Richie's voice comes from in front of us. My head whips his direction. I hear a clanking sound from beside me, and I know TJ dropped something from his hand.

"No!" Both of us shout at the same time. Peeking around a corner, Richie cocks his head slightly, his eyes squinting like he's not sure what to make of us. I freeze up, TJ scrambling to stand next to me again.

"Nope. No boners here. I mean, not talking about boners. Of course no one would have one, but we weren't talking about it either."

I roll my eyes at TJ. That wasn't totally obvious, or anything.

"You guys coming, or what?" he asks.

I wait for TJ to go first, which he does, and Richie leads us into his living room.

It's a badass room with a huge big-screen TV on the wall, with three different video game systems below it. I'm thinking there are probably other things in the room as well, but I'm too distracted by the massive game collection to care.

It's like I have no say over what my feet do as they head toward the games. "Holy shit."

"Nice, huh?"

"Definitely." I look over because I don't recognize the voice to see a guy with red hair standing next to me. "Hey," I say to him.

"Hi. I'm Dave."

"Bradley."

Dave hits me in the arm. "If we have time afterward, we can all play a game or something."

My eyes must light up at that because Dave starts laughing.

Figuring it's not too cool of me to admire electronics and games while TJ is setting up, I head over to help him.

I don't have to ask him any questions this time as I get the tripod and camera angled toward the couch. It's like I'm more a part of it when I know what to do, and that makes my chest swell when I didn't expect it to.

TJ gets his laptop going before he grabs the mics, handing them over to the guys.

Everything only takes about ten minutes before TJ and I are seated in chairs, Richie and Dave on the couch. He goes through his speech about being natural blah blah. Richie and Dave nod and lie back on the couch, relaxed.

TJ counts down before hitting power on the camera, something he's never done. He avoids my eyes when I look at him, cementing my guess that he's trying to look a little more professional in front of Richie and he doesn't want me to know it.

A strange wave of annoyance washes through me. Maybe I was sidetracked by the guy's looks at first, but that's because I didn't expect it. TJ knew. And now that I'm paying attention, I notice his nose is crooked and he has a chip in his tooth. Unfortunately it doesn't take from his looks, no matter how much I want it to. I'm sure TJ doesn't find anything wrong with him either.

"Why don't we start by you both introducing yourselves," TJ tells them. Dave actually goes first, followed by Richie. After giving their names, they tell us the name of the college they go to.

"Sports or anything?" TJ asks them. I find my gaze on TJ instead of the duo, watching him in his element. He sits up straight, fully concentrated. Confident. I'm pretty sure I'm that confident on the court, but it still kind of makes me feel awed to see TJ so strong and comfortable about who he is right now. All the time actually.

"I wrestle," Dave says.

"Are you out?" TJ asks while I sit back and observe him in action.

"Yeah."

He turns to Richie. "What about you?"

"No on the sports but yeah, I'm out. I have been since I was a freshman in high school."

"Was it a good experience or bad?"

Richie shrugs. "I was one of the lucky ones. I'm not going to say my parents weren't a little disappointed. Maybe that's not the right word, but they didn't expect it. They worried, and I was scared shitless to tell them, but I also knew they'd support me no matter what. There were little things here and there in high school, but in the grand scheme of things, nothing over the top. I grew up in the same Maine town my whole life. Everyone knew each other, and they knew me. It didn't matter there."

Richie's experience sounds close to mine, except I never sensed any disappointment from Mom.

"Were you worried before starting college? It's a different world. More diverse, which is good, but then you're in a new environment with people you *didn't* grow up with."

Richie bites his lip, looking like he's trying to form words. "Was I worried? Yeah. I think that's a natural response, but there's a difference between being worried and fear. Or being worried and caring. This is who I am. It'll never change, and that shouldn't mean I have to live my life any differently than anyone else. That I shouldn't have the same rights or, hell, the same comforts. I decided not long after I came out that I wouldn't accept being treated differently as a possibility for myself. No one else should either."

Dave smiles at him, setting a hand on the back of Richie's neck and holding it there. Comfortable. Natural.

Tilting my head a little, I look at TJ. That will be him. That *is* him. One hundred percent comfortable, and also doesn't care what anyone thinks. It makes the fire inside me burn hotter, the need stronger to be that kind of guy.

As though he feels my eyes on him, TJ glances my way and grins. My stomach feels light, and I realize how much I like the experience when he's the one giving it to me.

His smile gets slightly bigger before his attention returns to Richie and Dave.

"And did things go as planned?" TJ questions Richie again.

Dave glances at the camera a few beats and then at TJ. "He came with a huge chip on his shoulder."

"I did. I guess I expected things to go bad, so I wanted to be prepared. I met Dave right off, and he knocked me down a few pegs. Then I joined the fraternity—"

"You're in a fraternity?" I almost don't realize the question came from me until three sets of eyes stare my way.

I lean back in the chair as Richie says, "Why does that surprise you?"

Now I feel like an idiot. "It doesn't. I mean, I was just curious. I just didn't know…."

"But it is surprising," TJ adds. "Maybe it shouldn't be and maybe it wouldn't be to everyone. Maybe it's stereotyping the typical college frat, but I think his shock is a natural reaction."

"No, no. I actually agree." Richie nods. "And maybe that's why I wanted to join in the first place. To prove I could. To show that I could have the same experience as a straight college guy—frats, parties, friends, relationships. We all know sports and fraternities can both have the mentality of the members being the best—the golden ones, or however you want to look at it. No matter how wrong it is, some people think weakness in regards to being gay. Different. So I guess the real reason I wanted to join is because I wanted to prove them wrong."

My thumbs start drumming on my legs again, and I don't know why. Still, every bit of my attention is on Richie. I'm hearing his words and dissecting them. *Different. Weak.* Those are words I don't typically think of when I consider myself. There are some differences with my friends, but the majority of the time, we see past it. Do other people see me as weak or different? I don't want to think they do. I don't want to think I've done the same thing, but I can see what Richie's saying too. He's like TJ. There isn't a weak bone in either of their bodies.

"And did you prove them wrong?" TJ asks him.

"Yes and no. How do you really answer that question? Like I said, I am who I am, and I'm here doing what I want to do. The guys in my frat are cool. We get along, and just like everyone in the world, we have similarities and differences. But do I think they look down on me because I'm gay? No, because they don't have a reason to. I'm just like them, and if someone does have a problem with it, that says something about who they are, not me."

Still holding Richie's neck, Dave pulls him closer. "It's impossible not to like him. Even if you don't want to, you do. It's just the kind of person he is."

I see what Dave is saying about Richie. I think of myself and wonder if the situation would be different for me. If I would be accepted so easily. And if I weren't, would it just be because of my sexuality or who I am?

Richie leans his elbows on his knees. "But the point is, any of us can do that. Dave's a gay wrestler. I'm the gay vice president of a fraternity full of straight guys. I don't deserve anything less than my dreams. None of us do. We just have to be willing to work hard to get them. I got here because it's what I want, and I refuse to accept anything less, just like you, D." He looks from Dave to TJ. "And you too. We've talked a lot about it, and you're the same. Wouldn't the world be a better place if we all were like that?"

Chapter 13

"WHAT'S UP? You've been distracted all afternoon," TJ asks when we're back in our hotel room.

"Nah, I'm good," I say. Dave and Richie were really cool. After TJ finished with the interview we hung out with them for a while, playing video games and stuff. It was fun, but TJ's right. I have been distracted, my mind studying and trying to make sense of how I feel about what Richie said, as though it's a test that if I don't pass, gets me kicked off the team.

"You're a crappy liar, sports guy."

Stupidly I grin in reply. "You're pushy, film boy."

Still, my body automatically flops backward so I'm lying on the bed with my feet hanging over the side. I rub a hand over my face, words finding their way out of my mouth. "He said you were just like him. Not me." And that's not the only thing that's been bothering me since the interview.

TJ sighs, sits and then drops down beside me. I move my hands under my head with my arms bent, and he does the same. It makes our elbows touch. My mind focuses on the feel of him and knowing he's there.

"He doesn't know you well enough to say who you are, or who you're not."

"But we both know he's right, and…." For a second I wonder if what I'm about to say sounds stupid. If it even makes any sense. It doesn't matter either way. Since I can't see TJ's face because we're both looking at the ceiling, it's easier to admit. "I don't know if I fully agree with what he said. I mean, yeah, we all want to be confident, right? And we should be who we are regardless of anyone else, but I also don't know that we should have to 'change people's minds' about who we are either. Or not take no for an answer. If someone doesn't like me, then I move on. They're not worth my time. I want to focus on who accepts me automatically." I think….

"I don't know if that's how he meant it. I'm not even sure I'm making sense." TJ's good at this kind of thing, not me. I don't get exactly what Richie meant, and I'm not sure how I feel about it. I don't know how to put my words together to sound as articulate as they do.

"I agree. We should refuse to take no for an answer and work hard to be who we are, but should we have to? Shouldn't acceptance just be automatic? Maybe the world would be a better place if people didn't have to work so hard to prove they're just as worthy as someone else and people just worked harder to accept everyone."

TJ doesn't reply at first. The longer I lie here the more my pulse starts thundering in my ears, the more my face gets hot. "Never mind. That was stupid." Pushing off the bed, I start to sit up, but TJ grabs my arm.

"That wasn't stupid," he says with all the confidence in the world.

I glance at him over my shoulder. "No?" The air in the room gets thick. His gaze on me makes me swallow deeply, before I lie back down. It feels too weird to be looking at him, to wonder what he's trying to find in me.

"No it's not."

"I just…. It's just hard, ya know? I think about Shaun, and it would be awesome if he had as much strength as Dave or Richie. But even if he did, the result would probably be different for him. Of course I wish he was out, but… I guess I don't think everyone can take the same path to get there, ya know?"

This time I don't wonder if what I said is stupid because it feels right.

"That's part of the reason I wanted to do this. We all share the fact that we're gay, but we all have so many different stories. Our lives are so different, just like everyone else's. We're each unique to who we are." He pauses for a second and then adds, "That was cool of you… putting so much thought into what he said. Sometimes I get so… like on a one-track mind about filming, that I don't let myself stop and really feel it. You did with Richie and with Shaun too. You're kind of a dick sometimes, but you're taking this more seriously than I thought you would." TJ laughs and I do too.

"Whatever." I sit up enough to push him. TJ rolls just a little but then grabs my arms. Falling back to the bed, I try to pull away but instead of getting free, he comes with me.

My body instantly starts going crazy—hot, jumpy, scared, and excited. One of TJ's arms crosses over my body, and he's leaning on the other one, so he's looking down at me as I lie on the bed. Did I mention excited?

My breathing is quick and deep, my chest rising and falling. He has to freaking feel it. Has to see it, and that makes me turn away because I'm so inexperienced in this. My stomach rolls. I hate the fact that I'm nervous about this. What guy my age is nervous about hooking up with someone?

I close my eyes when TJ uses his finger to roll my head so I'm facing him again.

"I threw up after I kissed someone for the first time," he says.

That makes my eyes jerk open. "That bad?"

"No. It was good. He was cute. But I was also drunk and scared out of my mind. Then I started freaking out and wondering if I did it right. He was older. That freaked me out more. Then my stomach started flipping around, which didn't go with the alcohol. I puked. He laughed, and I never saw him again."

"That would suck." I smile at him.

"It did. Are you going to try and kick my ass if I kiss you?" he asks.

My heart, stomach, every part of me starts to go wild again. "No."

"Puke?"

This time I only shake my head because that's easier to do than using words.

The nerves start falling away, and it's just that jittery excitement filling me up as he gets closer and closer. The second his lips touch mine, the nerves are totally gone. Or maybe I'm just too busy to pay attention to them.

TJ's lips are softer than I thought they'd be. Then his tongue is at my lips, and I realize I need to freaking open them. I do and he pushes in. His tongue touches mine, and mine his. I feel a little bit of roughness on his face that wasn't there with the girls I kissed. It makes me hungry for more.

I slip my tongue into his mouth, needing to taste him. He chuckles against me, but it doesn't make me want to pull back. I just crave him more. My body is screaming *hallelujah*, and I can't help but agree with it.

The callus on his finger brushes my abs, under my shirt, and I'm totally wishing I could feel his chest against mine.

My body keeps yelling *more, more, more!* while my head is saying, *chill, chill, chill.*

TJ makes the decision for me when he pulls back, smiles down at me, and then sits up. I do the same, rubbing my hands on my pants because they're sweating like freaking crazy.

"Did someone say boner?" He repeats Richie's question from earlier. A laugh breaks past my lips because he's totally spot-on. There's no reason for either of us to try and say otherwise, and soon TJ's laughing with me.

We fall back on the bed again, still cracking up. I don't know if it's really that funny, if he's trying to distract me, or if I'm trying to distract myself. But then I realize I'm not embarrassed. I'm not freaking out. I'm just having fun, and I think he is too.

It feels like ten years before we settle down, and then I sit up again, pushing the hair off my forehead. TJ's hand touches my back, and I don't freeze up at all.

"Are we gonna go to that party tonight?" he asks me.

Richie and Dave invited us to a party with people from their school, since we sort of hit it off today, and we're in walking distance.

I'm not going to lie and pretend I don't think it would be cool to party with a bunch of college people. "I want to, if you do."

"Of course I do. We have to be prepared for next year, right?"

At that I stand up. TJ's still lying down, and I hold my hand out to him. He grabs ahold of it, and I pull him to his feet.

"Thanks, sports guy."

"No problem, film boy."

Chapter 14

I HEAR the music from the street when TJ and I walk up to the party. The porch light is bright enough that I can see the grass is overgrown and there's a five-foot blow-up can of beer on the porch.

"I'm definitely thinking this is the place." TJ quietly chuckles and nudges my arm.

"There's a high probability you're right." I nudge him back. "Come on."

My legs are slightly shaky because of nerves. It's not like I don't go to parties back home but those are parties where everyone knows me. I'm not the odd man out like I will be here. We'll likely be the youngest people here.

TJ lifts his arm as though he's going to knock, but I wrap a hand around his wrist before he can. "No one will hear us if we knock. At a place like this you just go in." It's stupid, but I think that it's one of the first, if not the only thing that I've known that he hasn't. This is a place I'll be more comfortable than TJ... kind of.

One of his brows creeps up. "Are you the party master?"

"I am."

"Then lead the way." He nods toward the door but then adds, "Are we holding hands in there? Not that I mind, but I didn't think you'd be down for it."

I jerk back when I realize I'd lowered our arms but not let go of him. "Sorry."

"You shouldn't be," he says simply and then waits. Taking his cue, I open the door, the music blasting so hard it makes my heart shake.

Trying not to look as nervous as I feel, I lead the way through the overly packed house. It smells like alcohol, weed, and sweat as people dance, scream, and sing around us.

"Richie said they'll be in the room downstairs!" TJ yells in my ear, and I nod before hunting down the stairs to the basement.

The music is slightly more muffled down here but not enough to make it really matter, at least until I open the door to the basement. All my wires start short-circuiting as I look at what's pretty much a dream come true. Pool, air hockey, one of the basketball hoops like they have in arcades, pinball, and anything else a guy needs to be happy is down here. My legs aren't shaking because of nerves now, but excitement. And whoever lives here has the right idea. Who needs to take care of the rest of the house if you can put your money toward a room like this?

"You're buzzing." TJ laughs.

"And you're not?"

"Fill this room with camera equipment, and I would be."

The way he smiles makes my stomach roll. I'm totally into a film boy.

"Hey, guys. What's up?" Richie shouts as he and Dave walk over to us. He has his hand in Dave's back pocket as they walk. The room is filled with people. There's frat pictures and symbols all over the walls, but no one gives them a second look. Maybe it's wrong and judgmental, maybe I'm doing the same thing to these guys that I don't want done to me, but I have to admit, I never would have expected them to just be cool with Richie in their frat. Or Richie and Dave together.

"Hey!" TJ says to Richie. "Thanks for inviting us."

"No problem." It's Dave who replies. "You guys aren't driving, right?" he asks. After we shake our heads, Dave says he'll grab us a beer.

Richie kisses him good-bye before Dave disappears through the crowd. We talk for a few minutes while we're waiting for Dave to get back. When he does, he gives TJ and me each a red plastic cup. "Come on." Dave nods, grabs Richie's hand, and starts to lead us through the bodies of people dancing and playing games.

I weave my way around bodies, and when I do, TJ puts his hand on my lower back, guiding me. It's a reflex to pull away. The second I do it, I wish I hadn't. It's okay to have his hand there. I *want* to have it there. In front of us Richie and Dave are holding each other, and it doesn't matter, yet my instincts to keep my distance are still there.

Opening my mouth, I try to figure out what to say, but then TJ just rolls his eyes with a small smile on his lips. *Okay.* He must realize it was a reflex, so I let it go, and we continue to follow Richie and Dave.

"We have a little more space here." Richie leans against the wall, and Dave rests against him with his back against Richie's chest. We're in one of the back corners of the room where not as many people are congregating.

Fidgeting, I shift my weight from my right foot, to my left and back again. Watching them… it just feels so normal. It's something the guys back home would do with a girl and something they're obviously used to doing with each other. It's something I want—just to *be,* to not worry about anyone else except for the person I'm with.

My eyes dart toward TJ, but he doesn't return the look. I search for a way to explain it to him but don't come up with anything, no matter how much I want to.

"So do you guys feel like you got everything you needed from us today? We're around if you have any other questions or something." Richie glances at me over his cup of beer.

"Not me." I point to TJ. "He's the expert. Ask him."

With a raised brow, Richie gives his attention to TJ. "Um… yeah." He stumbles over his words a little, which is a first for him. "I didn't get a chance to go through all the footage, but I think it's good. I'll send you guys a copy when I'm done and let you see it. Oh, I was thinking…."

TJ gets into TJ-film-boy-land so I let my attention wander around the room. A couple guys are shooting baskets as the timer winds down. The pinball table dings as some girl hits the top of it, obviously pissed.

"Wanna go play?" Dave asks.

Both TJ and Richie shrug their shoulders, leaving me to be the only person to say yes.

Another group hits the basketball hoop, so I lead the way to one of the empty pool tables. "You any good?" Dave asks.

"I can play," I reply.

"I suck," TJ adds.

"You guys don't know this but Dave sucks too. I'm pretty much the king of pool. Dave gets pissed because it's one of the few things like that I kick his ass in. To make it even it'll be me and TJ against the two of you."

"Works for me." TJ grabs a cue and the rest of us do the same.

The game goes pretty quickly. Richie wasn't lying when he said he's good. He and TJ kick our asses. Well, Richie does at least.

"Come on, the hoops freed up." I push my way through bodies trying to get there before anyone else does. They file in behind me, and we play a few rounds. I win them all. From there we hit up air hockey and a few video games, and the longer we play, the more I realize that I really need to try and get my own house in college so I can build a room like this.

Dave challenges me in every game we come across. Basically we stop to drink more beer, but that's the extent of the pauses. I'm three cups in and feeling a little woozy when I look around us and see that Richie and TJ are gone.

"Where'd they go?" My eyes scan the room for TJ.

"They got bored. I'm sure they're around here somewhere. Wanna go find them?" Dave downs the rest of what's in his cup before setting it down.

"Yeah."

One trip around the room, and we realize they're not in the basement anymore. Dave heads toward the stairs, and I follow, my legs feeling a little wobbly. We're partway up when he asks, "Are you with him?"

My stomach rolls, but I think it's more the alcohol than the question. "No...."

Dave smiles. "But you like him."

And I do. I don't really know why because we're totally different, but I do. "Yeah." I shove my hands into my pocket. "I've never...." Biting down on my bottom lip, I try and figure out what I was going to say. No, I know what I was going to say, but other thoughts start crowding in—does he like me as much as I'm starting to like him? Will I scare TJ away with my indecisiveness? Will he get sick of me?

We're in the kitchen by now, and it's thinned out a little. Dave looks at me, nothing but understanding. He's only a few years older, but we both know he's a million miles farther.

"He's the first guy I've ever really liked. I mean, I knew I was gay, but I've never...." Dizziness hits me, and my palms sweat.

Dave lays a hand on my shoulder. "We all have a first. Doesn't matter if it's a crush, relationship, or sex. Doesn't matter if you're straight or gay, either. We all have a first and there's nothing wrong with that."

"Not at eighteen."

"So?" he asks. "Age doesn't matter."

With my head down, I kick at my left foot with my right. "He kissed me today. That sounds stupid. Forget I said that." Who talks about a kiss like I just wanted to? People I know do it all the time, but that's bragging, talking shit. I actually want to *talk*.

I try to turn, but Dave grabs my arm.

"It took me four dates to kiss Richie, and he wasn't even my first. The nerves are worse when you really like someone."

"Yeah?" I ask him, making eye contact.

"Yeah. And fuck... it gets better. You have a whole lot of fun firsts ahead of you, man." Dave winks at me. Suddenly, I'm not embarrassed anymore. What I *am* doing is thinking about the fun I'll have with all those firsts he's talking about.

"I just... I feel stupid because I haven't done all this. And I haven't even gone out with a guy. I'm out, but it's still hard."

"We all have to go in our own time. TJ gets that, even if you don't realize he does."

"I mean, it's not like.... I'm still learning about him." About myself.

Dave laughs but not in a way that makes me feel like shit. It sounds like he's been where I am before. "Come on, Bradley. Let's go find your guy."

Even though TJ's not mine, I like the way it sounds. My guy....

Chapter 15

THE BACKYARD is almost empty when Dave and I get back there. There's a couple making out by the pool, one in a swing and another on a table.

Dave's elbow bumps my side. "There they are."

He walks toward the other end of the pool, and I notice TJ and Richie sitting on the end with their pant legs pulled up, and their legs in the hot tub. TJ's making swirls with his, and I imagine his leg has to be bumping against Richie's each time it does. The alcohol in my stomach suddenly feels much more uncomfortable there than it did a few minutes ago.

They bailed on us without a word—what? So they could come out here and talk alone?

Dave reaches them before I even get my legs to move. He kneels next to Richie, kisses him and says, "Hey, baby."

"Hey, you. Done playing games now?" Richie replies.

"We were getting bored, but now I'm tired. Are you ready to go?" he asks Richie. I'm still standing away from the group, still watching, but TJ hasn't turned to look at me once. What the hell?

Dave stands and helps Richie up before TJ pushes to his feet too.

We take the side gate so we don't have to walk through the house again. TJ and I still haven't said a word to each other. Dave and Richie are holding hands.

When we get to the street, Richie says, "Which way are you guys?"

It's TJ who answers. "To the right."

"We're the other way. Keep in touch, man. Let me know how it all goes. I can't wait to see it." Richie lets go of Dave to hug TJ, and I cross my arms.

"Take my number, Bradley. If you ever want to talk or something." Dave waits as I pull my cell phone out. I'm sure he has better things to do than to talk to me, but it's cool that he's offering. He's doing it because he knows I'm still working through things.

After I put his number in my phone, he takes mine.

"Bye, Bradley. It was nice to meet you." Richie shakes my hand, and then he and Dave head the opposite direction as us.

It's about five minutes into our walk before TJ speaks. "I'm pretty freaking buzzed."

"Me too." For something to do, I avoid stepping on the cracks in the sidewalk when the lights make them visible.

"You have fun?"

"Yeah." Without my instruction, my feet stop moving. "Thanks for bailing without saying a word."

One side of TJ's mouth rises almost in a sneer, making me wish we weren't standing under a streetlight so I couldn't see him as well. "We were bored. Why's it a big deal?"

I don't know.

But I can't make myself say that, and I can't find the words I'm looking for either. It was a party. I almost never spend a whole party with the person I went with. It just doesn't work that way. But we also both know that TJ's into Richie and... "Holy shit. You're jealous." TJ's words interrupt my thoughts.

"What?" *Yes.*

"Yeah we both think he's hot, but it's not like he's not happy with Dave. Plus, you seemed pretty into Dave."

Wait? What? "I'm not into Dave."

"Regardless, Richie and Dave are together." TJ takes a few steps and then stops. I'm not pissed anymore, just confused. What's going on? "I don't get you, Bradley. You're *out.* Everyone's fine with it. You let me kiss you today, but then you freak out because I touch your back around people and then get pissed because I stuck my feet in the hot tub with some guy you think is good-looking? Are you okay with being gay or not? Are you *really* out or not? Do you like me or not? Dude, make up your mind and stick with it."

Thoughts bombard me like a battering ram, trying to break in. Trying to break me down. *You're right. I don't know why I'm freaking out. I like you.*

But those are words, and I'm tired of words. I act stupid and then apologize with little other action.

TJ tries to pull free when I grab his wrist. "Don't go."

"Why?"

I pause for a minute and then decide to just go for it. He's so strong. All the people we've met are stronger than me, and now it's my turn. "Because I'm going to kiss you."

TJ stops fighting me. His hand grabs my wrist as I still hold on to him. His mouth drops open in surprise, and I don't realize it until I'm moving in. He recovers quickly, his tongue finding its groove with mine.

I take another step toward him, grabbing his waist. My foot accidentally comes down on his. He tries to back up, but the weight of my foot on his makes him start to go backward. It makes us both go backward as we fall into the grass and then we're laughing. Laughing and kissing and all the strength is boiling inside me.

We're in the same position as we were earlier, except I'm on top this time. I'm leaning over him, and I'm kissing him as grass rubs against my arm.

Pulling away a little, I look down at him. The light reflects off his crazy-blue eyes, and I touch the spikes on his head, and TJ pushes the hair from my forehead, but it just drops back in place.

Maybe it's the alcohol or maybe I'm high on him, but I roll off TJ and onto my back. My eyes find the stars, and I think I would take the time to try and count all of them if it kept us in this moment. But it's not enough. I'm so stoked I did this. Not, TJ. Me. *I* kissed *him*.

Pieces of one of our conversations race through my head—when he told me one day I'll be able to say I knew him. My mouth pops open, and I yell, "I just kissed TJ Bennett!"

It's like my body doesn't know what to want or feel. Part of me feels all hyped up, embarrassed I just yelled that, but then there's a voice in my head reassuring me that we're lying in the grass, no one can see us. Cars are driving by, but there's no one else here.

"I think you're more drunk than I thought," TJ says from beside me.

"My friends know I'm gay, but they think it would be weird to see me with someone."

He doesn't call me on the fact that I didn't reply to what he said.

"I know it shouldn't be like that, but it's one of the things I worry about. It's kind of like what Richie said, I guess. He refuses to feel uncomfortable or refuses to let his sexuality keep him from having something he wants, and I'm scared it will. Or I worry what people will think. Sure they may know, but it would be different to see...." *I may know too, but it's different to act on that knowledge....*

"Are you ashamed? Like, really ashamed?" TJ doesn't look at me. Maybe he's looking at the same star that I am.

"I don't know…. Maybe."

With that TJ leans up on his elbow. "You're so different than anyone I've ever met. You have this pride that made it so you had to come out. Like you had to do it because you believe it's what the right thing is. Did you *want* to come out, though?"

"I wanted to show people I'm okay with who I am."

"Are you?" he asks.

TJ leans back a little when I sit up. He does the same, both of us sitting in the middle of someone's yard with a busy street in front of us.

"I'm getting there." We stare at each other for what feels like an eternity. TJ snaps a picture of the sky, then of me. "I wanna kiss you again." Now that I've started, I don't know if I'll ever want to stop.

"I'm right here," he answers.

So I lean in. My hand feels cold against his warm face, but all that's forgotten when our lips press together again. When TJ moans, I moan, and I realize I really like kissing TJ Bennett.

I press my lips to his once more. Then the corner of his mouth—then I laugh. "You look all dazed. I must be a good kisser."

TJ shrugs, looking more serious than I figured he would. "You're the kind of guy who's good at everything he does, I think."

He almost sounds sad when he says it, which I don't get at all. "Says the eighteen-year-old guy who's making a documentary that could possibly save lives. I never woulda done something like that. I think my mom's obsessed with you. Every time we talk, she says how cool this is, and how proud your parents must be. You've scored me major 'good son' points," I tease.

TJ pulls at the grass for a second and then rolls his eyes. "I'm sure you didn't need this for your mom to be proud. She loves you. You wouldn't be here right now if she didn't."

He's right about that. I wouldn't have been here if she didn't push. My mom is pretty badass. She's strong. I've always wanted to be like her. "I think she might be part of the reason I came out. Didn't want to lie to her, ya know? Not about something that important."

With his finger, TJ starts tracing letters or pictures on my thigh. "Yeah… yeah I want to make mine proud too."

"Pfft. Whatever." At first I move to teasingly push his hand away but decide I don't want it gone. "You're Mr. art-gallery, documentary-making, creation-myth-class-taking guy. I think you nailed the make-your-parents-proud thing."

"Well, I *am* pretty awesome." He drops his hand, but I grab it. He's been way cooler to me than I deserve. The whole time we've known each other, I've been an asshole to him off and on.

I've always been determined. When I met Chase and he was good at ball, I wanted to be good at ball, and I got it. Right now I decide I'm done being lame. I'm just going to be… me.

"I know I'm a jerk sometimes, but I'm working on it… and you are, awesome I mean." Okay, totally time to stop rambling now.

TJ must realize I'm feeling like an idiot because he stands and says, "Race you back to the hotel."

Without a word, I push to my feet and start running.

Chapter 16

As TJ pulls onto the street, I grab his phone and look at the screen. "Philly, huh?"

"Yeah. Depending on traffic and how much we stop, it could take anywhere from seven to nine hours, probably."

"Okay." I set his phone down. "I can drive part of the way if you get tired or something. I'm thinking drinking the night before we had to leave probably wasn't the best idea." By the time we got back to the hotel last night we were both beat and passed out almost the second we got there.

There's a small chuckle in his voice when he says, "No shit."

We drive for a few minutes before TJ says, "What's your favorite color?"

Um... okay. That was random. "Blue, yours?"

"Gray. Every time you see a blue car heading the same direction as us, you get to ask me a question. When I see a gray one, I get to ask you."

"Because neither of us would answer questions otherwise?"

He shakes his head as though that was the most ridiculous question in the world. "Who cares? This way is more fun. That's what matters."

Like always, TJ's right. There are times I look at him and wish I could be more like him—be the person who will do anything or say anything and stand up for anything. Be the guy who's always honest even if people don't like it. He looks at things totally different than I'm used to. He's always been cool to me even when I wasn't to him, but he doesn't take shit either. I've never seen him look down at someone or heard him talk bad about someone.

I envy that.

"Okay, let's do it." It doesn't take long before I spot a blue SUV passing us. "There's blue, so I get to go first. What's your real name?"

His lips stretch thin, though I'm not sure he realizes it. "Thomas Joseph Bennett III, at your service." There's a little sneer in his voice that I've never really heard from TJ before.

"Why does that sound like a bad thing?"

This time he looks at me when he speaks. "Do I look like a Thomas Joseph the third to you? Come on. It's way too stuffy for me. I'm going to make artsy, creative films. Thomas Joseph sounds like I'm going to be an accountant or something."

"Holy shit." My stomach hurts I laugh so hard. "You're going to be an accountant. With a name like that, it's pretty much a guarantee." I totally can't believe he's insecure about this. TJ's not insecure about anything, yet he is with his name?

"What do you mean funny? Funny how? How am I funny?"

"Whoa. Channeling Joe Pesci from *Goodfellas* there?"

TJ's head whips toward me. When he does, he takes the steering wheel with him.

Hoooonk!

"What the hell?" I yell as TJ jerks the steering wheel the opposite direction and gets us in our lane again. The guy in the car one lane over flips us off as he speeds around us.

"You've seen *Goodfellas*?" he practically screams.

"Dude, you almost just killed us and you're asking me about a movie?"

With his eyes firmly planted in front of us, he speaks. "People our age usually haven't seen *Goodfellas*."

I cross my arms feeling a little lame. "I like older gangster movies. What's wrong with that?" He starts to turn his head, but I say, "Eyes on the road."

I can see the smile on TJ's face, even though he's not looking my direction. "Seriously, man, you've never been as hot to me as you are right now. I love gangster movies."

My face warms as I shift in the seat. I've never had a dude call me hot before. The heat spreading through me isn't unwelcomed, though. It's almost like fuel, making me feel a little hyped. Totally not going to get all weird about it, though. TJ's always so calm and put together, while I'm the one who's always freaking out about something. I want the kind of calm, the kind of confidence he has. "Gangster movies do it for you, huh?"

"Guys who watch gangster movies do it for me." His brows go up. "What's your favorite?"

There's this little twitch of excitement in my chest. I don't often impress TJ, and as embarrassing as it is, I realize I want that.

"*Goodfellas* is one, of course. But *Donnie Brasco* is badass. *Reservoir Dogs* is great and I freaking love *The Untouchables*—what?" I ask when I notice TJ staring at me like I have two heads. "And watch the road, remember? We want to live to get this documentary made."

It takes him a second before he speaks. "You didn't say *The Godfather* or *Scarface*, sports guy."

"Was I supposed to? I mean, I like them, but you asked what my favorites were."

"No, you definitely weren't supposed to say them, but everyone does. Which is fine. They're incredible films, but they're not my favorites either. Have you seen *Once Upon a Time in America* or *Mean Streets*?" he asks, that buzz in his voice he usually only gets when he's talking about his documentary.

"Nope."

"Dude!" He reaches over, grabs my leg and shakes his hand as though he can't keep from moving. "We gotta watch those. You'll love them. I have a shit-ton of movies I bought downloaded to my laptop. I'll see if they're there."

"You're excited."

His hand loosens, but he doesn't pull it away. "Excitement isn't a strong enough word. I don't have anyone to watch gangster movies with, and you'll love these—oh nice. Gray car. I get to ask you a question now."

"Are you on drugs?" I tease because of his rapid topic change.

"Funny. No trying to stall, though. Hold on… let me think." He pulls his hand away, and I instantly want it back… until he holds his chin, thumb on one side, and fingers on the other, rubbing like he's deep in thought. Then I can't help but laugh.

"Tough question, huh?"

"This is serious business. Questions are important because the answer forms how you perceive someone. Your mind automatically makes assumptions, and even if you want to, those are hard to change. And who even knows if that person is being honest and they're telling you who they really are? Regardless it doesn't matter, once something is in your head…."

My feet automatically move to rest on the dashboard. I go to pull them down, but TJ says, "It's okay."

Now he's got me tripping out over a stupid question because I want him to like what he sees. I want to tell him who I really am, if I even know who that is. "Save us both the worry, then, and ask me, like, my shoe size or something."

"No way. That will be too easy on both of us."

I don't know how this could be hard on him, but whatever.

He's quiet for a few minutes making me hope he can't think of something. Finally he opens his mouth, the question "What are you afraid of?" falling out.

Sinking a little lower in the seat I wrap my arms around my knees. "What do you mean?"

"I mean anything. Afraid of bees? You can say that. Afraid of playing basketball in college, or going to college, or the color red—"

"People are afraid of the color red?"

"There's someone who's afraid of everything, Bradley. What are you afraid of?"

It sounds like such an easy question. What am I afraid of? I'm afraid of big boats. I can pretty much promise you that I'll never go on a cruise in my life, and I'm not real fond of heights either, but that's not what TJ means. I know it. The thing is, I want to be real with him. Give him something real because most of the time the things I give people are superficial. My friends are awesome, but they don't ask me questions like TJ does, and we don't talk about the important things TJ talks about. Which is cool. It would feel strange anyway, but here… here I think I can say anything and maybe it wouldn't be weird.

Like I always do, I let my thumbs drum on my legs as I figure out what to say. No, that's a lie. I know what I'm going to tell him. "Two things really—the first is something happening to my mom. She's great. Both Tyson and I would be screwed without her."

I pause, but he doesn't ask me the second thing. Somehow, TJ giving me the space and time I need, gives me the courage I need too. "I guess I'm afraid of being who I am. Not just the gay thing, but that's part of it. I'm nervous about actually going there, about actually *being* gay, even though I know I am. Does that sound stupid?" Instead of giving him time to answer, I continue before I am too embarrassed to keep doing this whole talking thing. "It's not just that though either. Sometimes I question everything I do, or think. I'm always worried about what people think of me, or if I'm doing the right thing, or if I'm being a douchebag, or acting like a pussy."

I shake my head. "God, I sound like an idiot." There's no blue car, but I still say, "It's my turn. What are you afraid of?"

TJ slumps as though his spine got shortened a couple inches, and he can't sit up straight anymore. "Of not making people proud. Turn on some music, yeah?"

For a minute I don't move. I just told him things I wouldn't tell anyone else, and he gives me a short reply before changing the subject? As I sit here, I realize it might be okay, though. Maybe it wasn't as easy for him to admit that as I assume things always are for him.

Without replying, I scroll through his iPod until I find something I like. Neither of us speaks again as we listen. The whole time, I wonder if he's sitting there thinking about his own fears, as well as mine, the way I'm thinking of my own and his.

Chapter 17

"ARE YOU hungry?" TJ asks a couple hours later. "I need to fill up."

"Yeah, and I gotta take a leak." He pulls off the freeway, and I add, "I got lunch... I wanna buy you lunch." I'd said I'd buy him dinner the other day and haven't yet. This time I'm not letting the opportunity go by.

"Works for me."

His response bugs me slightly, and then I feel like a douche. What do I want him to do? Jump up and down because I want to buy him a meal? "Like a date, buy you lunch. Which I guess is kind of stupid since we've been in a car for three hours while we're on a road trip together but...." My first thought is *but what,* followed quickly by *what the hell was that?* Dude. I can't believe I just said that. How lame am I?

But then TJ nods with a small smile and says, "Okay. I'll go on a date with you." With a quick glance my way, he winks. "And I won't even try to hold your hand in public."

There's a part of me that knows he's not trying to be an asshole by that. He knows I'm mixed-up when it comes to this, and I can see he's trying to be reassuring without getting all serious again. We've had enough serious for today, but still the words feel like nails on a chalkboard in my ears. I don't want him to have to try and make things easier on me. I don't want him to have to worry about holding my hand in public.

The first restaurant we notice is a TGI Friday's. It's not until we're pulling in that I think about the fact that all our lunches, except the one at that mall in Ohio, have been fast food. He probably wanted to hit a drive-thru, and I didn't even think about that.

"If you don't want to—"

"I want to."

"Okay." I shrug, but I'm really thinking *me too.*

We head to the restaurant, and I open the door for him when we get there. TJ walks in, tells the hostess two, and she seats us. I run my hands down my legs as I sit, trying to wipe the sweat off them.

"Bradley?"

As soon as I look up at him, he snaps a picture.

That's not the first time he's randomly taken pictures of me. "Want evidence of this moment for the rest if your life, huh? The first time Bradley Collins bought you lunch."

He laughs and then puts his feet up on the booth next to me, leaning back. "Something like that. *First* time, huh?"

Whoa. I totally said first. Because there will be more.

"Can I get you guys something to drink?" The waitress hands us menus and saves me from rambling my way through whatever I would have said. I've never rambled in my life until I met TJ. The guys would give me shit beyond belief if they heard me.

"Just a Coke," I say.

"Same here," TJ adds.

"Okay. I'll be back in a minute to take your orders." Her blond hair flies as she turns and speed walks away. Her hips sway back and forth when she does.

I don't know what makes me ask the question, but softly I say, "Do you ever wish you were into girls?"

TJ looks at me over his menu. "That's a hard question. There's a part of me that knows things would be easier if I was, but I don't want to change it. Seeing her does nothing for me the way seeing you does. Why would I want to change that?"

Okay, so here's the thing. I know he isn't just talking about *me* specifically. Yeah, he's attracted to me, and I'm attracted to him. That's obvious, but still it makes my heart slam and my body feel light. For years I've known who I am, and who I like; but for years I've never done anything about it. Never given myself the opportunity to meet someone. I've watched girls go all air-hearts-and-crazy over my friends, or even me. I've been around my friends talking about girls, and hitting on girls, and making out with girls, and rehashing tales of sleeping with girls, but now I'm on the other end of it. I'm the one who's having someone flirt with me, and I can finally flirt back.

It's almost like I've robbed myself of that part of my teenage years. That's what it's supposed to be about, right? Experiencing, and kissing, and breaking up, and breaking hearts, falling in love, and hooking up. Yeah maybe I'm not doing all of those things, but here, on this trip, I have some of them.

"Yeah… yeah, me either. I don't want to change me. Maybe I have before but…." It's not me.

We both order burgers and fries. We talk a bit while waiting for our food, but TJ spends some of the time texting or playing on his phone too. Once the meal is done, he pushes his plate away from him and leans back in the booth, his ankles still crossed beside me on my bench.

My phone buzzes in my pocket, and I jump a little. After pulling it out, I see a text from Mom.

Hey, you. How's it going?

My mom's the only person I know who uses complete sentences and the correct punctuation and words when texting.

good. eating w/ tj. U?

She replies quickly. *Oh! I don't want to interrupt. I'll let you finish. I love you. Call me when you get to Philadelphia!*

I'm pretty sure I have the only mom in the world who would actually hope her son would fall for someone on a road trip with no parents. Not that I think she wants me out having sex, but yeah… if I came home and told her TJ was my boyfriend, she'd probably throw a party.

"Your mom?" he asks.

"Yeah."

"I need to call mine tonight too. She's excited to hear how things are going. She's curious about you."

"Me?" I ask. "Why?" My hands start sweating again as I look around the room. The restaurant isn't too busy—people eating, talking, and working, no one paying attention to us.

"Umm… I don't know. Your mom would be interested in a guy you were going away with for two weeks, wouldn't she? Don't tell me your mom didn't ask ten million questions about me."

He's got me there. "At least yours didn't demand to meet me." Because yeah. I might have freaked about that. My first finger twitches as my hand rests on my leg.

"You wouldn't have been ready. It would be a dick move not to get that."

It's those words that make me lift my hand. Those words that make me put it on TJ's shin. Those words that allow me to feel the roughness of his hair on my palm. That make me rub my thumb and just sort of… feel him.

TJ doesn't speak. Doesn't move. Yeah, I know no one can see me, and I know what I'm doing isn't a big deal, but it so totally doesn't feel like it. It's like last night when I was buzzed, only today I'm sober. The waitress could walk up or someone could sit behind us. Maybe I would jerk my hand away if they did and maybe I wouldn't, but it's not dark and we're not in a hotel room and I'm not altered like at the party, yet I'm touching him.

"You totally like me." TJ's voice is full of laughter, yet not mocking. It's quiet, and I know that's for me. Know him trying to make me laugh is for me too.

"You totally like *me*." He still has his feet up next to me, and my hand still rests on him the way Jabbar's would with that girl he's seeing or Chase's would with whoever his hookup of the week is. Like Henry and Matt, or Richie and Dave would do if they went out to eat together. The way Shaun would love to do. The way I'm stoked to touch him.

"You're growing on me, sports guy."

With that, my eyes meet his. "You're growing on me too, film boy." Really he got it right the first time. I totally like him, more and more every minute.

Chapter 18

TJ COMES out of the bathroom in our hotel room, and nods when he sees me on the phone. "I'm going to grab some drinks and ice while I call my mom." He speaks quietly as though he doesn't want to interrupt my conversation with my mom, even though she hasn't answered yet. I don't know why, but I find that cute.

"'Kay. See ya in a minute." After we had lunch earlier, I didn't have the balls to hold his hand when we left, but I kind of figure that's okay. And I think he did too. I drove the rest of the way into Philly, and then we had picked up some fast food before coming to the hotel. I took the first shower, and he grabbed the second one. I'd expected him to start screwing around with the footage we've shot so far, but he didn't.

"Hey, you." There's nothing but happiness in Mom's voice.

"Hey. How are you guys?"

She talks a little about work and how Tyson is staying with his best friend, which I'm sure he's stoked about. Mom's friends with his mom, so I'm sure she's trying to help out since I'm gone.

We don't have a whole lot to talk about because I told her about Dave and Richie after our interview with them, and before the party that she knows absolutely nothing about. I plan to keep it that way.

"What are you guys doing tonight?" she asks.

"I'm not sure. TJ usually messes around with his camera or laptop all night, but he said something earlier about watching some movies. He's into gangster stuff too. He has a few he wants me to see."

So, maybe it's uncool to know your mom as well as I do, but it's the truth, and as soon as I say that, I know her mind is running wild with questions and assumptions she's not sure she should spit out or not. Talking about a guy with my mom is pretty much one of the top three things in my life I never want to do, so I say, "Don't ask, Mom."

"Blah. You're no fun. You're having a good time, though? You're experiencing a lot?"

Even though she can't see me, I nod. "Yeah, it's been cool. We talk to people who are so different, and it's... I guess it helps me to see...." I have no idea what I'm trying to say. "I guess it helps me see that I'm just like everyone else. Or can be, or...." I had it in my head that gay is supposed to be one way—who even knows what that way is—but there is no one way to be a gay person just like there's not one way to be anyone else.

"Oh, sweetheart. Of course you are."

I love her for what she wants to do here, but again, talking with my mom about some stuff is just strange. "TJ said we might not be able to meet with the guy we're supposed to see tomorrow until the next day. He'll let us know in the morning. I swear he started twitching when he found out. He's totally into this stuff. He cares about his documentary the way I am with sports, only times it by ten thousand. He's really into art and architecture stuff, so if we have to postpone a day, he'll probably drag me around to do stuff like that."

Mom pauses so long that I say, "Hello?" to make sure she's still there.

"Bradley... I know you don't want to hear this, and maybe I should have talked to you about it before you left. You're eighteen. I'm not stupid. I know what kids do, and I just want you to know, I'd rather you not do anything but if you do... just because there's no risk of pregnancy, you still need to be safe."

What. The. Hell?

The phone almost slips out of my hand, and I stupidly let my eyes dart around the room like TJ came back in without me noticing and heard what she said. "Mom, I'm not talking to you about sex."

"Well I'm talking to you about it."

O-kay. I'm now doing what's probably number one on the list of things I never want to do.

"You like him. I hear it in your voice, and I love that, kiddo. I want you to like him if he's a good guy, but don't rush, okay? I know you're on this trip with no supervision, and you probably feel like you can do anything, but remember that this is the first boy you've ever had a crush on. I just don't want you to try and do everything because you feel like you should, or you have to, and then regret it, okay?"

No, there is nothing about this conversation that is okay. I'm not going to pretend I've never thought about sex because, hello? I do. But I'm also not going to front and pretend the idea doesn't, as fun as it sounds, freak me out too. "Mom, I'm not having sex with TJ!"

Karma is really being a jerk right now because TJ walks in right as I say that. His eyes get big and then he busts out laughing. He must have forgotten the door because it starts to close on him, hitting the bucket of ice out of his hand and making it fall to the floor. The bucket isn't enough to stop it either. TJ looks down, obviously shocked by the ice falling, and the heavy door smacks him in the forehead.

"Oh, shit," I say.

"Don't curse at me, Bradley Michael."

"I'm not! You made TJ hit himself in the head with the door."

"How did I do that?" she asks.

Pushing off the bed, I jog over to him. Mom's rambling in my ear, I'm caught between being worried about him and embarrassed for myself, and the whole time TJ doesn't stop laughing.

Finally, after explaining to Mom what happened, I get her off the phone. First, I grab some of the ice that isn't on the floor and wrap it in a washcloth. "For your head." I hand it to TJ, who's lying on the bed with a red lump in the middle of his forehead.

I clean up the rest of the ice and tell him, "I'll go get more." He opens his mouth, but I stop him before he can get the words out. "Please don't ask."

He's amazingly still smiling, even though his head has to hurt. Before grabbing more ice, I run down to the shop in the hotel for a bottle of Tylenol. I don't know if they carry it, but I sure don't, and his head can't feel too good.

A few minutes later, I carry the ice and Tylenol into our room.

"Can I ask now?" he says the second I walk in.

"No."

"In an hour?"

I smile. "No."

"Tomorrow?"

Seriously. He's killing me. "Maybe." Taking one of the sodas from the mini fridge, I hand it to TJ. "Here, I got you some Tylenol. Could you have a concussion or something? I know you're not supposed to go to sleep if you do." Maybe it's a long shot, but I know the door is heavy and hotel doors always close hard.

"Were we going to sleep? I thought we were having sex. I mean, it's a little soon, but I'm down if you are."

I drop my head backward but have to admit, I'm holding in a laugh. "Ha-ha."

"Ugh. Fine. But don't say I didn't offer. We're watching movies, though, right? I want to if you do."

"For sure. I know you said so earlier, but I didn't know if you would be busy, or whatever." I pull my phone out of the pocket of my basketball shorts and toss it to the bedside table.

TJ's looking at me through the curve of his arm as he holds the ice to his forehead. "Can you grab my laptop out of the bag? And the tray for it too so it doesn't get too hot."

I get them and when I do I see his smaller camera too. I pick it up and snap a picture of TJ with the pack on his head.

"Nice."

"You want your memories, and I want mine."

I hand the laptop and tray to him. TJ turns so he lies on his stomach on the bed, with the laptop in front of him against the headboard. This is one of those moments where I would have freaked out or gotten nervous before, but I fight it this time. Instead I walk to the other side of the bed and climb in beside him.

He slides the laptop over so it's in the middle of us, but still the bed is small enough that I feel him, feel the bed move when he does and smell his soap and wonder if he smells mine.

"Which one first?" he asks.

"*Mean Streets*," I say, not sure why I pick that one.

TJ searches through his computer, brings it up, and hits play. We're quiet through most of the movie. When it's been going for an hour and two minutes, I bend my arms, to rest my head on them. My elbow touches his, and I don't move it.

When the movie is over, I tell him how incredible it was—which is true.

"Wait till you see the next one. It's just as good."

Around the hour mark again, I glance at him, his eyes getting fluttery. "Hey." I touch his back. "Don't go to sleep yet. Give it a little longer, okay?"

He looks up, his head resting on his arms. There's his dimple when he smiles. "Thanks."

He's right about how good this movie is too. I talk him into *Donnie Brasco* afterward, partly because I don't know if he should sleep and partly because I don't want to move from his bed.

It's only about forty-five minutes into the movie before TJ falls asleep. Reaching over him I grab my phone and Google concussions. He said he had a headache (which anyone would after a blow to the head) but TJ's also a movie freak. The fact that he fell asleep watching one worries me.

It's been nearly six hours. He hasn't had any of the other symptoms, so I let him sleep. When the movie is over, I turn off the laptop. *Maybe I should stay up just to make sure he seems okay.*

Rolling to my left side, I watch him for I don't know how long. I should probably turn out the light, get back into my bed, but I don't do either.

TJ moans a little and rolls to his side. He stretches his arm out, resting his hand on my side. Without moving the rest of my body, I look down at his hand on me and smile.

Just a little longer. I'll stay up just a little longer.

Chapter 19

I LOVE sleep. Even though I have an alarm, Mom usually has to come into my room a couple times before I actually open my eyes. It's a process, I tell her, and then she laughs and tells me I'm crazy.

There was no process this morning. A good five minutes ago my eyes just popped open for no reason, and I haven't been able to close them since.

I'm lying on my right side, with my back to TJ. TJ who's sleeping beside me. Who slept beside me all night. Two pairs of muscular legs, wearing two pairs of basketball shorts. Back to chest, T-shirt to T-shirt. TJ who has his arm slung over my waist. TJ who has his face in the back of my neck, blowing warm air across my cheek.

I have to take a leak, but I don't want to move. Maybe he'll roll over before he wakes up and not know he slept with his arm around me.

Maybe I don't want him to.

"I sleep with a body pillow." Breath and words across my cheek.

Well, I guess he's awake. "Huh?" To roll over or not to roll over? I don't know.

"It's black. I've always slept with one. I guess I'm a sleep-hugger. Sorry. I didn't mean to freak you out, or, like, invade your space. I must have thought you were my pillow."

First of all, I'm pretty sure I don't feel like a pillow. Second, he's still holding on and I'm still okay with it. And third, I don't want him to think I'm a pillow.

"I don't wanna be your pillow."

"O-kay." He starts to pull his arm back and roll, but I grab his wrist.

"No, I mean I want to be Bradley. Not the pillow." Which still makes zero sense. I want him to touch me because he knows it's me, but those words are a whole lot harder to say.

TJ must get it because he stops pulling away.

"How's your head?" I ask. "I stayed awake for a while because I was worried about you sleeping."

"Feels perfect to me. How does it look?"

Rolling to my back I look up at him. "A little bruised but not bad. Dumbass. I can't believe you let the door smack you in the head."

TJ laughs, rolls over and gets out of bed. "I walked in on you talking about having sex with me to your mom. What did you expect?"

So I don't have to look at him, I turn to get out of the bed on the opposite side. "She was talking about it. Not me."

"My mom might be understanding about a lot of things, but I think she would have a heart attack if she had to talk to me about sex." TJ opens his bag and starts to dig around inside.

"I'm sure it was just as awkward with your dad."

"Probably would have been. Maybe that's why neither of them did it. Good thing I'm handy with a computer." He looks over at me, grinning. Dude, he is seriously so good-looking. The more I'm around him the more I see it. It makes my whole body fill with heat.

"Let's just not make any movies about that, okay?" I tease him before I start to walk toward the bathroom.

"Hey." TJ nods for me to come closer, and I walk over to him.

"What?"

"I'm gonna take you somewhere tonight."

"You are, huh?"

"Yep. You'll like it." He takes a step closer, puts a hand on my waist. "As long as no one is around, it's okay to kiss you all the time now, right?"

Fighting to keep my voice steady, I say, "Well maybe not *all* the time. Our lips would get tired."

"Okay. Well just so you know, you can kiss me whenever you want. Or all the time if you want. I'm totally good with it. Tired lips or not, kissing is worth it."

A rock lands in my stomach. His face is all playfulness, so I know he didn't mean it as a slam that I have no balls. The feeling is gone as soon as he presses his lips to mine, though. There's no room for anything there except for all the *hell yeses* pinging around inside me. It's like my body wants to make up for lost time—for all the times my friends have hooked up compared to how many I have, which is, like, one. Just TJ.

He slips his tongue in my mouth, and I let him, then push my way into his, because I want to be the one kissing him. I want to be the one tasting him, and TJ lets me. His hand digs into my side, and I grab his, but then he's pulling away.

"I need a shower. Then I have to get ready for tomorrow. It's... it's going to be a tough one, man. And I want to be sure we have time to go do something tonight." TJ grabs his bag and then disappears into the bathroom. It's not until I hear the water turn on that I remember I still haven't gotten to take a leak.

"HOLY SHIT." The stadium in the distance is a total giveaway. "Holy *shit*," I say again. "We're going to a Sixers game?"

TJ laughs. "Dude, your voice just went up like two octaves. I've never heard you so excited. Yeah, we're going to a game. We don't have the best seats in the world, but we're going."

"That is so awesome. I can't wait. Who are they playing?" My eyes don't leave the stadium as we get closer and closer.

"I think it said the Bulls."

He thinks? *He thinks?* How can he not know? *Because he doesn't really care....* "Hey. Thanks. This is... I know you're not really into basketball."

"Eh." He shrugs. "You did art galleries with me, I can do a game. And it's not that I dislike basketball. It's just not my favorite thing. Or anywhere close to being one of my favorite things." He laughs. "I can appreciate sports just like the next guy, though. My dad and I used to go to a lot of football games when I was younger. It's always been big in our house."

"Used to? Why don't you go anymore?" I pry my eyes away from Wells Fargo Center to TJ. He talks about his mom often but almost never talks about his dad.

"He's too busy. He's one of those workaholic types."

"And you're not?"

"What? You're crazy, Bradley. I'm nothing like him. He's mister suit-and-tie, anything-arty-isn't-worth-it, a-man-is-measured-by-his-wallet, kind of guy."

Whoa. Totally didn't see that coming. "Well maybe you're not alike in that way, but you're both obviously responsible. You work like crazy on this documentary."

"Hmm, I guess."

"And maybe art isn't his thing, but at least he's supportive. He must think it's worth something because he doesn't care that you're doing this. Your parents are funding most of the whole trip."

He sighs, and pauses before continuing. "This documentary is important. It means something. He pretty much has to be proud of the fact that I'm doing it, don't ya think?"

He has me there. "Yeah, I guess you're right. Still, though, you're the most put-together person I know. It's not like your parents don't see that."

TJ stops at a red light and leans my way. "You're always giving me compliments now. I still can't believe how much you like me. I'm going to remind you of that every chance I get."

I shove his shoulder, and he laughs. "What about you? I'm a jerk to you half the time and you're still around. I still can't believe how much you like me."

"Well, you do like gangster movies. That makes it kind of hard not to. The whole basketball thing puts a little dent in it, though."

A car behind us honks, so TJ starts to drive again. Being around him is so different than I thought it would be. In a way it's just like chillin' with my friends. We tease each other and talk shit to each other, but with TJ there's the kissing.

And also the fact that even though TJ does dish out a lot of crap, he's also probably the nicest guy I've ever known.

"Hey." I set my hand on the back of his neck. "Thanks again."

"It's just a game, Bradley. It's not a big deal."

Yeah it is. "I don't mean just about the game… I mean everything. I'm sure bringing me with you wasn't real high on your to-do list, especially after how I acted at The Spot and everything."

He's quiet for so long, I don't think he's going to reply. He drives to the stadium, pays for parking, and finds a spot before turning the key, and looking my way. His voice is quiet when he speaks. "Maybe it seems like it, but I didn't do this for you. I did it for me. And I'm glad you're here… in a different way than I thought I would be."

This time I don't even scan the area for people before I kiss him. It may be in the privacy of his SUV, but I'm still counting that as a win.

Chapter 20

THE NEXT morning I'm still buzzing over the game. It was a close one, lots of good defense in the end. The Bulls won, but I was okay with that. I like both Chicago and Philly. For me, it was just the fact that I got to go. That I got to talk to TJ about basketball the way he talks about art or film or even creation myths.

He always seems to have home court advantage—he's been with guys before, and he's 100 percent comfortable in who he is—that it felt good to tip the scales in my direction, even if it was only for a few hours.

It made him seem a little less perfect, because we all know I'm not even close.

He's a little quieter as we get up and get ready today. He's still in his bed when I get out of mine, saying I'm going to grab a shower. Once we're both ready and we have the car loaded, we walk across the street to a coffeehouse to grab a quick breakfast.

It's not until we're in the car driving that he says, "I know I'm not supposed to tell you who we're talking to, but I feel like I need to prepare you for this one, man."

Aaaaand, just like that my thumbs start drumming, and my skin feels tight. "Why?"

TJ pulls over to the side of the road and takes a deep breath. "He's dying."

Whoa. That totally wasn't what I expected to hear. "What? How?"

"Lung cancer, though he never smoked. He's on hospice so he's at home. His husband is there with him. He was diagnosed six months ago. They're thinking he has a few weeks, maybe a month left. He stopped chemo two and a half months ago—wanted to be able to live before he died, ya know?"

No, no, I don't really know. I've never had someone close to me die. I've never known someone who knew they were going. "I guess." The air in the car suffocates me. We're going to see someone who's dying. It makes my throat feel full and my stomach ache.

"Hey." TJ reaches over and grabs my hand. He threads his fingers through mine and I study the way they fit together. "This, what we're doing, is important to Greg. We're giving him a voice about something that's close to his heart before it stops beating. We're giving him something that will last. We're making his story eternal. That's what I try and focus on."

The tightness in my throat starts to ease, but the ache is still there. I've always known what TJ is doing—what we're doing—is important, but I never thought of it that way before. But he did. Of course he did. I've never thought of half of the shit he has. "Yeah, I guess we are, huh?" With my other hand, I finger the bracelets on his wrist.

TJ nods. "Anyway, I wanted you to know. Do you want me to tell you what he's going to talk about?"

"No." The answer is automatic. I started this journey letting it unravel as it goes, and I want to continue to do that. Somehow I almost feel like I'll get more out of the experience that way. I hope the guy we're going to see today will get the most out of this too. "Come on," I tell him. "Let's do this."

"Yes, sir." TJ pulls his hand away, starts the car, and drives away.

It takes us about twenty more minutes to get to Greg's house. It's in the suburbs of Philly, a little white-and-blue, two-story house with matching homes all around it. It's funny how they all look the same. Driving up and down the street you would never guess there is a man dying in this particular home. I guess that's kind of true to life, though. No matter how something or someone looks on the outside, we never really know what's going on inside. Never know if they're dying there or suffering without a word.

My hands shake a little as I help TJ unload things from the SUV. Why am I freaking out so much over this? I don't even know the guy.

"Hey, we got this, sports guy. It's not a big deal."

But it is. "We're telling his story. He's dying, and we're telling his story. That's huge, TJ. I just… I don't want to screw it up."

He cocks his head, his eyes getting that far-off look that I call his zone. The one he gets when he's working because he's concentrating on it, this thing that is so important to him. Only now he's looking at me like that. Concentrating on me as though he's trying to solve me. "What?" I ask. TJ's never looked at me like this. I feel his eyes on my skin. It's tripping me out, but I also sort of like it.

"There wasn't supposed to be more to you than what's on the surface. I didn't think this would end up being important to you."

There's a part of me that wonders if I should be offended by that, but somehow I'm not. I'm honored. "It is. All of it."

"I know." And then he raises his camera and snaps a picture of me.

"Stalker," I say, trying to lighten the mood.

"You like it." TJ grabs his last bag from the SUV before slamming it closed.

His arms are fuller than mine, so I'm the one who rings the bell after we step onto the porch. A few minutes later I hear the locks click before a guy opens the door.

He's tall, with blond hair, looks like he's maybe in his forties. I expected older.

"Hey, guys. Let me help you with that stuff." The man takes one of the bags from TJ. After closing the door behind us, he leads TJ and me to a table and sets down the bag. TJ puts down his stuff as well, so I do too.

"It's so great to finally meet you." He shakes TJ's hand.

"It's great to meet you also," TJ replies to him, then looks at me. "This is Bradley. Bradley, this is Jeff."

"Hi. Thanks for letting me come. I'm sorry for all that you and Greg are going through." My words sound so superficial. They're standard, script in a way, the kind of thing everyone says, but I mean them to the marrow of my bones.

Smiling, Jeff shakes my hand. "Thank you, and we're glad to have you. This is important to Greg. He wants the world to know about Darren's story, so many of our stories, so we're grateful that you guys wanted to include him in your film."

I have no idea who Darren is, yet I nod. And I like the fact that he called it our film and not just TJ's.

"I'm going to check on Greg and make sure he's awake. If so, I'll come and grab you guys and we can get started."

"Who's Darren?" I ask TJ when Jeff steps out of the room.

"I can't tell, remember?" he winks. I know he's trying to keep the mood light, so I roll my eyes at him, attempting to do the same.

We wait for a good five minutes. The whole time I'm nauseous and hot. My hands feel jittery as I think about the fact that we're about to see someone who is dying. TJ jumps like four feet when Jeff opens a door to the room he went into and tells us to come back.

I let TJ go first, which he does easily, leading the way into the room. There are two huge windows, both with the curtains pulled open. Against the wall between them is a hospital bed, tubes and machines everywhere. Tubes all over the man lying in the bed.

TJ walks right up to him, and I linger a little behind. He looks old, way older than Jeff does but a quick scan around the room tells me it's the poison in his body making him that way. There are pictures of him and Jeff everywhere, where Greg's hair is black instead of his head bald and his eyes are bright instead of dim. He's solid instead of frail. *Chill out, chill out, chill out.* I can do this. I need to do it. I want to.

TJ leans down and hugs him, Greg saying something only TJ can hear. After a minute he stands up straight and then signals me over. "This is Bradley, the guy I told you about. Brad, meet Greg."

Greg's thin eyebrows raise, his voice soft and broken when he says, "The Bradley, huh?"

Whoa. TJ has talked to him about me? I'm assuming it was before we left... "If he's spoken about me, it probably can't be very good." I chuckle, but Greg shakes his head.

"We all have good parts and bad parts. That's what makes us human. There's always both, and there's no use in talking about the bad if we don't care about the good."

When my eyes find TJ, I see his face red for the first time. "Greg's a good listener." He shrugs.

"I have quite a bit of free time on my hands nowadays. Jeff bought a good speaker for the phone so I can lie here and talk. Can't die in the middle of a conversation. I think that's against the rules." Both TJ and Jeff chuckle, Jeff walking over to hold Greg's hand. The hand of the man he loves, the man who's suffering. I trap the words I want to ask in my throat. How can you joke about dying? How can Jeff joke knowing he'll lose Greg?

"Nothing will change it," Greg says as though he can read my mind.

I feel stupid, but I still say, "Isn't it hard, though?"

"Every second of every day. Sometimes laughing is the best way to deal with death."

Jeff leans forward and kisses Greg's forehead. For the first time since we started this road trip, I wonder if I'm going to be able to hear the story.

Chapter 21

"THE NINETEEN eighties were a unique time for those of us in the gay community."

"How so?" TJ asks him, and Greg chuckles.

"How long do we have? I could go on for days. We were coming into our own, learning to be proud of who we were and not hiding it. The bigger cities were the most active. I lived in New York at the time and the gay scene was alive and thriving, though fighting as well. We were tired of being invisible, which made things exciting." Greg's voice sounds stronger than it did earlier. There's a steadiness he didn't possess when we first came in. I see the struggle in him, the need to do this well. The need to proudly tell this story from his past, whatever it is. Right now he's not a man lying in bed with cancer. The tubes and wires somehow disappear, and he's just a man fighting to do something that's important to him. I'm even more honored to be here as I watch him.

Greg's voice is a little softer, a little sadder when he adds, "And then we started to get sick."

My muscles freeze up and harden, making my body stiff. This is about HIV. AIDS. I might not know a lot about it, but I think everyone knows the eighties were a pivotal time. We all know that's when AIDS really came to the forefront and a lot of people lost their lives.

"Before we get into that can you tell me about what you were doing personally at that time? Before the epidemic really hit, I mean." All TJ's attention is solely on Greg. I've seen him in his zone before but nothing like this. It's in the stiff way he sits and the set of his jaw. A bomb could go off in the room, and I'm not sure if he'd notice. None of us has once glanced at the camera.

For a brief second, Greg's eyes sparkle. "Having fun." Those words linger in the room. From the seat beside Greg, Jeff reaches over, rubbing his hand on Greg's forearm. "Darren and I had just taken off from the small Kentucky town we were raised in. It hadn't gone well when he came out to his family, though we knew it wouldn't. My family was more understanding. Darren's family told him they wanted nothing to do with him—wanted him away from me.

"There were a lot of tears in my household, a lot of, *can't you try? Just find a woman, and after a while you would grow to love her.*" Greg shakes his head. "People don't get it, especially back then. I couldn't be with a woman. I didn't want to be with a woman. They said they would always love me, and I knew they would. They supported me, Darren also. They became the only thing he had that resembled a family, but the worry and even anger was always mixed in."

"Why were they angry?" Neither Jeff nor I have said a word so far, and I doubt either of us will. TJ is too good at this for me to have anything to add, and I see the determination in Jeff. He wants to give this to Greg.

"Because I couldn't be straight. For a while they thought I just wouldn't."

TJ nods. "So you left?"

"We did. My family helped a little bit. We took off in Darren's 1967 Volkswagen Beetle that was on its last leg. We had—maybe—five hundred dollars to our name. We had no jobs waiting for us, but we didn't care. We were going to be free, and we had each other. That's all that mattered to us."

Greg's eyes close briefly, but there's a small smile on his face too. *What is he seeing?* I wonder. And then… the strangest thing happens. I see a picture—two guys, in an old bug… just driving. Feeling free like he said. I've never experienced not feeling free. Yeah, I've tied myself up because of my own stupid issues, but I'm not trapped. Not by others at least. It's only me who traps myself.

"And you went to New York?" TJ asks him.

"Yep. The car broke down twice on the way. We would have just left it and gone, but we didn't know if we'd have to sleep in it for a while."

Live in it?

"You look surprised by that, son." Greg turns his attention to me. I almost shake my head and say it's nothing but decide to share what I'm thinking.

"It's just… you sound almost happy as you say that. Like sleeping in your car would have been good memory."

"Not would have been. It was. It was an adventure for us. We were in our early twenties. We'd felt trapped our whole lives, and now we weren't. Sleeping in a car couldn't put a damper on that."

Trapped. I don't know why I focus on the fact that he used the same word as me.

"It's hard to explain what it's like. If there were any other gay people in our hometown, they weren't out with it. Until I met Darren I felt completely alone in the world. I knew no one else who was like me and everything I heard from others was so negative. People who were my friends would hate me, *hate* me, if they knew who I was. Then I met this incredible man who didn't think there was anything wrong with me. He was like me."

Even though I try to divert them away, my eyes find TJ. TJ who is like me. The first person I've ever known who is. It's more than twenty-five years since Greg met Darren and yet in some ways, our struggles are still the same. Mine not to the same extent of his because I had more options. But I still never took them.

My chest gets tight as I realize I feel lonely too. I've always felt lonely. I have family and friends who know yet in so many of the ways that count, I've been alone.

"My mom tries to talk me into going to this center for gay kids, but I never wanted to go." I pause, trying to control the conversation just so I can make sure I'm really the one who spoke. I don't usually share things like this. "I didn't think I needed it. TJ's the first openly gay person my age I've ever known."

"You're out?" Greg asks.

"Yes. Kind of… I mean, I am, but I'm still trying to be okay with it. Shit, maybe that's not the right word. Oh, sorry for the language. I probably shouldn't say that." For the first time today, I glance at the camera. I shouldn't be saying any of this. It's Greg's story, not mine.

"I'm sorry," I say again, trying to stand.

TJ's hand on my leg stops me midstand. It's Greg's "You have nothing to be sorry for," that makes me sit down. "It'll never change. Who you are will never change."

My head tilts down, gaze in my lap. Looking at TJ's hand there. At the string bracelets on his wrist. "I know." And I don't want it to. I really don't. "I just don't want it to be a big deal." *Then why do I make it one?*

"Most things that matter to people are a big deal to them. That doesn't have to be a bad thing. Mold it into the kind of big deal you want it to be—like this. What you're doing. It's a good thing and *that* is a very big deal. Who we are, gay or straight is always a big deal, son."

I nod, but I'm not sure if I'm really letting the words seep in. Not sure if I want them to in this moment. It might be something I need to do alone. "How long did you have to stay in your car?" Silently I beg him to answer my question, to turn the attention away from me because it's too much right now.

"Not very long at all." As Greg speaks, TJ takes his hand back. "I got a job at a bar and Darren at a restaurant. We got a hole-in-the-wall apartment in NYC. It's hard to put into words the way it was then. We were young and stupid. We were in love and experiencing life for the first time. Needless to say New York City is nothing like Kentucky. The city became such a huge part of who we were. We lived and breathed it. It was like an addiction, pumping through us because it was full of possibility—a possibility we never really thought we would have. Even if it was just walking around the city all night—which we did a lot, we wanted to experience it all."

"The eighties were a big time for drugs. Was that part of it?" TJ asks him, and I'm thinking, *holy shit I can't believe he just said that.*

"Drugs were everywhere—gay or straight, but we didn't need that. We had each other, and we were living. That was enough for us. God, I wish you guys could have known him. All of you." His movements are slow as he turns toward Jeff. "You couldn't know Darren and not love him. He loved everyone. He was happy and energetic, and he wanted to do things that mattered in a way I wouldn't have wanted without him. We used to work in soup kitchens and help feed the homeless. All Darren wanted to do was give back, be who he was, and have me."

He shakes his head, and when he does, I notice moisture glistening in his eyes.

"That's all he wanted...." Greg mumbles.

But he didn't get it. Even without Greg finishing the story, I know he didn't get it.

Chapter 22

"GREG, MAYBE we should take a little break. You guys don't mind if we take a breather, right?" Jeff eyes TJ, who responds immediately.

"Absolutely not. We can hang out here or come back in a little while if that's easier."

Before TJ even finishes speaking, Greg is already shaking his head. "No. I don't need a break. I want to keep going."

"Are you sure?" I ask him, worried. His voice is rough now, tired, and his eyes are still wet.

Instead of replying, Greg goes straight into his story again. "I wasn't as good as Darren. I'd always known, but it became more and more obvious as months went on. New York was so much more than I ever expected. The city was exciting and liberating. There were men, so many men, and they were incredible and experienced and I'd never known anything except for Darren."

"You broke it off with him?" I interrupt, just as TJ opens his mouth to speak.

"No. I didn't have to do that. I would never have to do something like that when it came to Darren. He knew me too well, and he always, always would have given me anything. He would have done anything for me."

Greg takes a few deep breaths before continuing. "That's why he broke up with me." When Greg raises a hand to his mouth, it's shaking.

Jeff leans over the bed, his mouth close to Greg's ear. "Take a break. You deserve it."

I'm on the edge of my seat, knowing Greg needs to stop but wanting nothing more than to hear the rest of his story. Nothing more than to talk to him. In all the other interviews, I was aware of the camera. Now, I couldn't care less about it. This is about Greg. Greg, Darren, and Jeff.

To Jeff, Greg says, "I'm good," before facing TJ and me again. "God, I loved him. I know it might not sound like it, but I did. I do. He was everything I could ever hope to be. And he knew it. Knew how much

I loved him and he loved me just as much. Giving your heart to someone doesn't magically make you incapable of making mistakes. It doesn't make you any less human, it makes you more human and whether we like to admit it or not, most of us are tragically flawed. I know I am."

"So, he just let you go?" TJ asks. "And you let him do it?"

"Yes and no," Greg replies. "We always knew we would get back together, and he told me that. I remember his exact words as we spoke that night.... *We came here to experience the world, we came here to be free, and I won't be the one to hold you down."*

"It was about sex? You wanted to be unattached?" TJ questions Greg.

"It wasn't only about sex. In a way maybe I did feel tied down. I hate to say that, but lying doesn't make it any less true. I wanted to experience everything, and Darren let me."

"What else did he say?" I ask.

Another pause from Greg. When he speaks, it's with his eyes closed. *"You love me too much to ever do it. You love me too much to go behind my back. Have fun. Meet people. Don't think I believe for a second it's permanent, Gregory Phillips. You're the man for me, and we both know it."*

It's so strange listening to him speak. Goose bumps travel up my arm. It almost doesn't sound like Greg's voice. Somehow, I think it sounds like Darren. Darren who I've never seen or heard. Darren who has to be dead.

"I'd never even gone on a date with anyone other than Darren. I knew I was gay since I was young. I never tried dating girls, even when I was in the closet. I met him when I was seventeen. We hid our relationship until we were twenty-one and left for New York. We were all each other knew, and even though I knew Darren was who I wanted, I felt this need to know what was out there at the same time."

"How long did it last? The breakup?" TJ leans back in his chair, crossing his arms.

"Six months. We still spoke all the time. Every day. I rented a room from a friend and let Darren keep the apartment. It got old quick, but I was scared to go back to him. Scared because I knew he did this for me and... it felt wrong. Being apart from the man I loved felt wrong, but did I deserve him back after letting him go?"

He looks older than he did when we first began. He sounds more tired than he did in the beginning.

"So you didn't go back to him?" TJ asks Greg.

A smile stretches across the man's lips. "Like I said, he was always better than me. I didn't know if I deserved him, but I knew I loved him. I knew he loved me, and there was nothing out there that I'd experienced that could hold a flame to him."

TJ and I are both quiet. I think the whole world is quiet while we all wait for Greg to continue.

"He came back to me. And somehow, we were even happier than before. We'd seen what was out there and knew what we wanted. I moved back in with Darren, and we let ourselves thrive again, not just on the city, but on each other. We volunteered because he loved it. We'd go to the theater, because I fancied myself somewhat of an actor. We didn't have much money, but we made do. We felt invincible. It was perfect." Tears fill his eyes again but none of them fall. His voice is broken when he speaks. "And then everything changed when Darren started getting sick."

I hear the rasp in his breathing. Hear my heart beating down my rib cage. Feel it breaking as my throat tries to close up.

"Goddamn it!" The tubes attached to him get tangled as Greg rolls to his side, away from us but toward Jeff. He's shaking, and Jeff leans toward him as Greg tells him, "I think I need that break now."

My legs are wobbly, and so is my heart.

"I'll meet you in the kitchen," Jeff tells us before leaning close to Greg, and whispering in his ear.

I stand first, but TJ is right behind me. We quietly slip out of the room, closing the door behind us.

As soon as we get into the kitchen, TJ asks me, "Are you okay?"

The word *no* lingers on my tongue, but then I really pay attention to TJ. His eyes dart around slightly frantic. He rubs his hands together, nervous in a way I've never seen him. So, I step closer. And closer again. "I'm cool. Are you?"

"Yeah." He gives me such a fake smile, I almost call him on it, but he starts speaking before I can. "I'm good. They're probably going to be a while. I'm going to take a walk. Text me if they're ready for us."

He turns, pauses, then faces me again. "Thanks, sports guy. You've been awesome." TJ presses a fast kiss to my lips and then disappears out the kitchen door, leaving me standing in the middle of the room, trying to figure out what just happened.

TJ is gone for forty-five minutes before I hear a sound in the house. Since it's coming from the back, I know it must be Jeff, so I sink back into my seat.

"Hey. Sorry about that. He's taking a nap right now. You guys are welcome to go and come back, or hang around. It's up to you." Jeff steps up to the coffeepot and begins making some.

"TJ went for a walk, so I guess we'll hang out." Why wouldn't he tell me where he was going? He's so easygoing, so together that I'm not sure what to make of the way he bailed. "Is Greg okay?"

He stays by the pot as though it will stop brewing any second, when it just began. "Yes. Is TJ?"

"I think so. We're not... I mean, he wouldn't have any reason to tell me one way or another."

Jeff has a small smirk on his face when he says, "Now that's not true. Even if you were only friends he'd have a reason."

"How do you know we're not?" Are we? I don't even know.

"I guess I don't. Maybe you are. Are you?"

The answer comes automatic. "I don't know." Which is true. Yeah we might have messed around, and we've both admitted to liking each other, but in reality that doesn't mean anything. It's not a promise of anything, I mean. I'm still being lame half the time, and it's not like kissing someone means you're with them. Chase would have a lot of girlfriends if it did.

Still the words don't sound right, as I replay them in my head. There's this swollen sort of feeling in my chest that says we're more than friends. "Can I ask you a question?"

"Let me get my coffee first," Jeff replies. "You want some?"

"Sure."

We're quiet as he makes two cups, cream and sugar, and then comes to sit at the table with me. "Shoot."

But now that I have the chance, the words are stuck in transition— my brain, my throat, my heart, I'm not sure where. I just don't know if it's the kind of question I should ask.

"You want to know where I fit into this whole thing with Greg and Darren, right?"

Wow. He's good. In a way it's probably a stupid question. Darren has obviously passed away. It's been a long time, so Greg would have moved on but.... "The way he talks about him."

"That's because he loves him. Would you expect any differently? Just because someone dies, Bradley, doesn't mean you stop loving them. You have to move on, but you always love them."

More truth. I'm not emotionally stunted enough not to understand but…. "I get it, but… isn't it hard?"

Jeff takes a sip of his coffee. "No, because I know Greg loves me. And I love him. He's not the first man I've loved either."

I nod, feeling stupid. "Yeah, yeah that makes sense." But there's more. Darren must have gotten AIDS…. Greg was with him…. And now Greg's with Jeff. What does that mean for them?

"Greg isn't positive and neither am I. But that's all I'll say about that. It's Greg's story to tell."

Shame makes my insides twist. "I'm sorry. I didn't mean—I hope that doesn't make me a jerk, being curious."

Jeff's cup makes a soft clank when he sets it on the table. "Curiosity doesn't make you a jerk. Only how you respond to the answer gives you the possibility for that. How would you respond if I'd said we were? Would it make you worry about drinking that coffee I just made? Feel uncomfortable being in our home? Those are the things that really matter."

And that's when I know I really am a jerk, because I'm thankful when the door opens. Thankful when TJ comes back in, not only because I was worried about him, but because that means I don't have to contemplate what my answer to Jeff would have been.

Chapter 23

IT'S BEEN three hours, and Greg is still sleeping. Jeff makes lunch. The three of us sit down to eat ham and cheese sandwiches and chips. Other than that we don't do much.

TJ gets on his laptop for a while, and I watch a little TV. Jeff tells us we can go but doesn't seem to mind when TJ says he'd rather stick around.

Jeff hardly lets fifteen minutes go by at a time without checking on Greg. It makes me wonder if my parents were ever that way. If they were still together, would Mom be everything for Dad that Greg is for Jeff? It's pretty obvious Dad wouldn't have been that to her. He couldn't even stick around.

"How'd you and Greg meet?" I ask Jeff when he comes back into the living room after checking on Greg.

"We met when we were both going to group counseling. It was for people who lost someone they love. We bonded over that, just friends in the beginning. It wasn't long after he lost Darren so neither of us were ready. It was about… oh, I guess four years later before we realized we were in love with each other. Sometimes, I almost feel like I knew Darren as well. We would talk for hours on end, in the beginning."

I want to ask Jeff whom he lost. If he lost the person to AIDS the same as Greg did, but then, we're not here for his story. I don't want him to feel obligated to share if he doesn't want to.

"I think he's awake." TJ peeks his head around the corner. "I was going to the restroom, and I heard him."

Jeff and I both scramble to our feet, but he says, "Let me make sure he's ready before you come in."

Duh. I should have thought of that. I sit back down.

"Sorry I bailed earlier." TJ leans on the arm of the couch.

"It's cool. You're okay, though?"

"Yeah. It's just sad."

"It seems kind of unfair, huh? Greg lost Darren and now Jeff has to lose Greg. It's shitty."

TJ smiles and pushes a hand through my hair. "You're cute when you're sweet, sports guy."

Warmth spreads through me hearing that, but then something else pops into my mind. "Then I'm probably not cute very often." Unlike him. I suck in a deep breath before continuing. "You're cute all the time, film boy."

"What?" TJ shoves me softly. "Look at you trying to show me up. Who knew you had game?"

I roll my eyes. "Yeah, I'm like a pimp."

We're both laughing when Jeff comes back into the room. Both of us quiet instantly. It almost feels wrong to enjoy myself right now.

"You guys ready to continue?" Jeff asks.

I wait for TJ to reply. This is his gig, and of course he says yes, so a few minutes later we're in Greg's room again, as he lies in his bed. Jeff takes up his vigil beside him.

Greg doesn't need any prompts before he starts speaking in his gravelly voice again. "It was right in the beginning of the epidemic. They were still calling it 'the gay cancer' and GRID, which stood for Gay Related Immune Deficiency."

"What?" sort of jumps out of my mouth. "Gay cancer?"

"Yes. The first cases were gay men, and then later it was drug abusers. They knew nothing about it. All they knew was gay men were getting sick and dying. It made homophobia worse. People wanted nothing to do with the gay community. They were afraid of us. They were afraid of getting sick. But at the same time, what was the big deal that we were dying? It was just the gays and the druggies. We were disposable. We weren't worth fighting for."

Sadness coats Greg's words, drips off them, and into me, landing in my chest.

"Eventually they realized you didn't have to inject drugs into your arms or be gay to get it. You just had to be human, but by then it had gotten out of control."

Jeff squeezes Greg's hand.

"So Darren was infected during your six months apart?" TJ asks him, professionally. But I see it in him, see the slump of his back and the tightness in his jaw. He feels the despair of it all. He feels it probably more than me.

"One person...," Greg whispers. "He'd been with one person in the six months we were separated. It was more than that for me. It shouldn't have been him." Greg's voice wavers.

"Did he have safe sex?" TJ asks.

"TJ—" I start, but Greg cuts me off.

"No, it's okay. That's what we're here for. Yes, he did. He wouldn't have lied to me, but condoms aren't a hundred percent either. And sometimes they break, or come off. We had safe sex with each other, but I never got it...." He shakes his head. "I never got it." After a few minutes of silence, Greg asks, "Jeff, can you raise the head of my bed a little more?"

And he does, making it so Greg sits up even more. He rubs a hand over his face and takes a deep breath as though trying to prepare himself. My breathing is fast, short, almost painful gasps as I wait. Wait and hurt for the loss I know he's going to tell us about.

"I can't tell you how many times I prayed to trade places with him. How many times I wanted to go back—back to before I was selfish and wanted my freedom because if I hadn't, Darren would have never gotten sick."

"You couldn't have known," TJ tells him.

"That doesn't matter," Greg replies. "It doesn't make me any less responsible for my part in it." He rocks back and forth slightly. "It progressed quickly. The gay cancer became HIV and then AIDS. More important people started getting sick so the government started paying attention, but it was too late.... Do you know he still made me go volunteer? Even when he was alone in the hospital, he would make me go once a week."

"Did his family come and see him?" TJ asks.

The pain slides off Greg's face, as his jaw sets. "No. They thought it was his punishment for being gay."

"Your family? You said they became like family to him."

Greg shakes his head. "People were scared. Everyone was scared. We were dying and the way people coped, the way they tried to ensure they wouldn't get sick too, was to forget about us. To stay away. He had me, and I had him, just like it had always been. Just us, and we found a way to deal with it together."

Water pools in Greg's eyes again, yet he still doesn't let it fall. Tears roll freely down Jeff's cheeks. Mine are trapped inside me, trying to break through.

Alone. Dying. Alone. Dying. Alone. Dying. I can't stop those words from running circles in my brain. The same way Shaun is alone too, except he's living with the loneliness. "No one? Not even friends or anything?" I ask.

"A few of our friends stopped by a couple times. Some were in their own room, down halls from Darren, or in other hospitals scattered around the city, trying not to die, and losing. Others were too scared they would be next. Fear is a powerful emotion, Bradley."

Yes, it is. I think about the things I'm afraid of—my friends thinking it's weird seeing me with a guy, someone staring at me if I walk down the street holding a boy's hand, of being the very person I am, the person I will always be, the person everyone who knows me knows I am, and it all seems so petty. So weak, compared to the worries of others.

Reaching over, I grab TJ's hand. Without a pause, he threads his fingers through mine.

"He never blamed me," Greg says. "Do you know how hard that had to be for him? He knew he would die, and I wouldn't, yet he never blamed me. He loved me until the end."

Greg looks down, away from the camera. "He started sleeping more. There were days I only saw his eyes once or twice. I didn't leave his side in the end, even to go volunteer. I couldn't."

Jeff's quiet weeping mixes with Greg's words. TJ's grip on my hand tightens so much it hurts, and I know I'm squeezing him with just as much strength.

"One day he woke up. He looked at me so deeply, the Darren I hadn't seen in so long that I almost thought he was cured. That he was a miracle and the nightmare was over... but then I saw it. He knew he was going. I said I was sorry, and he said he loved me. I told him I loved him too, and he told me to be safe, to be happy. I don't know if I believed he was really going anywhere or not, but I told him the same. Then he closed his eyes, and I held his hand as he died—just him and me. We were all each other needed."

Greg turns to Jeff. "Open the drawer for me, please."

Jeff does, and he knows exactly what Greg is looking for. He pulls out a picture of a black man in his twenties. He has his arm around a young Greg, and they're both wearing the biggest smiles I've ever seen.

"We've lost thousands and thousands of people to AIDS, but I wanted everyone to know about this one. Darren Nicholas Hale, the best person I've ever known." And then he looks at Jeff. "Jesus, I got lucky. I got to love two incredible men, even though I'm not sure I deserved either."

Jeff kisses his hand and tells him he deserved them both. And I know he did.

We're quiet as TJ and I clean up the equipment. My chest is hollowed out, yet somehow full at the same time. My hands shake, but I don't try and hide it. My thoughts travel back to the girl I'd stepped away from at the secondhand store and the question Jeff asked me earlier—if it would matter if either of them were positive or not.

"Hey, do you know if we have any local groups or organizations that help with AIDS stuff back home?" I ask TJ. "I mean, I know things are better now but—"

"I'm not sure. I can check." One side of his mouth kicks up as though he's holding back a smile.

"If so, do you want to maybe go help at one? Or if not, even volunteer at a homeless shelter or something." It's such a small thing but something I want to do. Something the old me never would have thought about. "I think Darren would like that."

TJ doesn't hold back the emotion on his face this time. "I think that would be awesome."

"I do too," Jeff adds.

Once we have our equipment packed away, we go back into the room to tell Greg good-bye. TJ goes first, and I wait outside the room for him. When it's my turn, I stand by the end of his bed and say, "Thank you. I...." My throat feels full. I can't make any words come out. I don't know what would come out anyway. I just feel like I need so say something. Why can't I say something?

"It's okay, I get it."

As I look at Greg, I realize he does. He gets it more than I do. Maybe even gets me more than I do.

Leaning forward, I do the strangest thing. I hug him. In my heart I know I'll never see Greg again. That probably is true of most of the people we've met on this trip, if not all of them, but it's different with Greg. Soon, no one will see him again. "You deserve them both" are the last words out of my mouth before I walk from the room.

"Hey." Greg's voice stops me at the door. "You do too. Whatever you're looking for, you deserve it."

My eyes start to burn, but I manage to keep from crying. With one last look over my shoulder, I tell him. "I'm trying," before walking out. When I get outside, Jeff is standing by the SUV, TJ inside it.

We shake hands. I start to open the door but then stop myself. "Before, you asked me if it mattered. It doesn't. Before this trip, it would have, but not anymore."

We don't say a word to each other the whole way back to the hotel. Once we're in the room, TJ takes his phone and says he's going to go for a walk to call his mom. As soon as the door closes, I dial mine.

"Hey, you," Mom answers, but I'm crying too hard to reply.

Chapter 24

IT'S AN hour later when I get off the phone with my mom. TJ isn't back yet. Part of me is grateful because it's totally obvious I've been crying. I don't want to look like a wuss in front of him, but then, I think maybe it wouldn't matter. What we did today—what we heard—was major. I can't get Greg's face out of my head. Can't get Darren's or Jeff's either. Greg's voice whispers in my ear, and it makes me think of myself. Of choices we make and how we never know the outcome of them. How one decision can change the trajectory of our lives.

And how wasting time is a really stupid thing to do. You never know how much of it you will have.

Shoving to my feet, I stumble trying to get to the bathroom. Quickly, I wash my face so I don't look like such an idiot, and then I grab my jacket and gloves before heading out the door.

My fingers screw up half the words I'm trying to text TJ so quickly. I have to delete most of it and start over. It's like I have this buzz under my skin—electricity that makes me feel wired, excited, scared, and a million other things.

I'm in the elevator when my cell beeps. *Walking back to hotel. Right around the corner.*

Stay outside, I text back.

I blame you if I freeze my balls off.

Laughing, I shove my phone into my pocket, knowing he'll wait. TJ's up for anything. He's fearless. I could probably ask him to do anything and he would. I always sort of saw myself that way, but I'm not. Not at all. I want to be, though. Want to be more like him. I don't want to have regrets.

The buzz in my skin gets faster and stronger the closer I get to walking out of the hotel. It's almost like when I had a little too much to drink the other night only this is all me. It's not some fake alteration, just Bradley.

Cold air hits me the second I walk outside. The Philadelphia street in front of me is packed with cars and the sidewalk is thick with people. I feel like I'm sucking energy out of them the way I do at a game—thriving on the people around me, pumping adrenaline through me, making me want to go faster and giving me more strength to do this.

"Going somewhere?" I hear from behind me. TJ's forehead wrinkles as he looks at me, probably wondering what I'm doing. Why I walked right past him and didn't realize he leaned against the building by the door.

"I'm gay," I tell him when I'm standing right in front of him.

The wrinkles in his forehead get deeper. "I kind of caught on to that."

"I don't...." I shake my head, not really sure what to say. Wishing I didn't have to use words at all. "I don't wanna screw up. I don't wanna miss out, but not in the same way as Greg." Greg let go because he wanted to explore. I wanna grab on instead.

I almost step back because this feels like crazy-cheesy-chick-flick territory, but I'm tired of stepping back. I'm tired of caring what people think. So instead of back, I step forward. Right between TJ's legs, and I grab his face wishing I weren't wearing my stupid gloves so I could feel him, but then just do it with my lips instead.

He's obviously sort of shocked because it takes a second for him to kiss me back. Then he does, and the people around us don't matter. This is a right—*my* right to kiss him—and I want to take it. To own it and who I am in front of all these people.

Someone bumps into my back, but it doesn't interrupt. I don't stop kissing. Don't stop moving my lips with his or my tongue from getting to know more of his mouth. My heart actually thumps harder, I stand up straighter when it's TJ who pulls away first.

"Okay... totally hot, but we don't want to get arrested either."

Smiling, I pull back, but he grabs my waist and says, "Give me a minute before you step too far back, okay?"

My smile grows so big my cheeks hurt. Standing where I have been, I grab his hand and lace my fingers with his.

"We couldn't do this in the room?" he asks.

"We could, but I didn't want to." I want everyone to see. "I... let's walk." I tug a little, but TJ doesn't move.

"It's cold, sports guy."

"So? I'll buy you a beanie. Let's go." This time when I pull, he follows.

"I'm kidding, ya know. I don't need you to get me a beanie for me to walk with you. It's kind of annoying that I like you so much."

I keep his hand in mine as we weave through people. "Have you ever dated someone who was…?" I don't want to use the term *in the closet* because I wasn't. I never really have been. "Stupid?"

"Oh God." TJ pulls his hand from mine and wraps an arm around my shoulder, pulling me close. "Are you sure you're not into film like me? That was pretty dramatic. You're not stupid."

My arm slides around his waist. "Yeah. I know." But I'm not sure what to call it. Human, I guess. "Have you ever dated someone who wasn't totally settled in with being gay?"

"Am I dating you?" he asks.

My eyes scan the people around us. No one is paying any attention to the two boys with their arms around each other. They all have their own lives and their own business and I know it might not always be that way, but in this moment, it is. "Yes." I want that. Want to be with TJ, not just because he's so put together but because he's cool and fun and honest in this way not many people are.

My stomach is in knots because he might not want the same thing.

"Then I have. Or I am. But you're hard on yourself. No one is totally okay with who they are. We all take a little work."

Except for him.

Neither of us talks for a few minutes as we keep walking down the street. I have no idea where we're going, but I'm not sure it matters. Just going *somewhere* is enough. "I can't stop thinking about them," I tell him. "Greg…. Darren… and Jeff. Greg's regret, but then if things didn't happen like they did, he wouldn't be with Jeff. But Darren died… he *died*. Alone."

"He had Greg."

"I know, but he didn't have his family. Or even his friends for that matter. I can't imagine. My mom would never do that. It makes me feel like… I don't know, like all these people have gone through so much shit to be who they are. Shaun, Greg, Darren, and what? I'm freaked because Chase thinks it's weird? It feels wrong."

"You should cut yourself some slack. We're young. We're supposed to screw up. We're supposed to be confused half the time. We all just do the best we can."

TJ and I keep walking, but I turn to take him in for a second. He looks like the same old TJ—the dimple, spiked hair, relaxed—but there's this sadness to his voice sometimes that I don't understand. I'm not always sure if I'm hearing it, but this time, I know I am. "Why are you doing this?" I ask.

"Because you wanted to walk."

"You know that's not what I mean."

"Because I love film. Because I think it's important." He takes his arm off my shoulder, but I grab his hand again. I'm not ready to let it go. Not just because I'm taking the step to really be public about this for the first time but because I like touching TJ. He makes me feel good. I always thought I felt okay, always thought I was happy and in tons of ways, I am. But being with him makes me feel like I won a play-off game I didn't even know I was playing.

"I was uncomfortable when I realized Greg's ex had AIDS... I was uncomfortable at the thrift store too. After hearing Darren's story.... God, I feel like such an asshole. I wanna go back to that thrift store on the way home. Think we'll have time?" What the heck I'll do when I get there, I don't know. It's important for me to go, though.

When TJ stops and looks at me, I almost turn to see if someone else is there, if there's something behind me because it's like he's never seen me before. Or like he's seeing someone other than me. I wonder who he sees and if he likes it. Wonder if it's the person I'm trying to be. "You're pretty incredible, Bradley."

People part around us as we block the sidewalk. I don't care if I'm in their way. I'm not moving.

"Seriously. My boyfriend is popular, good at sports, *and* a nice guy. All the gays will be so jealous." TJ smirks, making me laugh. There's this foreign twitch in my chest that I've never felt, but I like it.

"Come on. Let's be Greg and Darren for one night. Let's walk around for hours exploring the city." I smile at him.

"Okay." So we do. We walk and look at buildings and stop for coffee. TJ takes pictures of everything, including me. There isn't much talking. The weight of the day, of Greg's story, still bears me down. I think it does with TJ too. It's after midnight when we get back to our hotel. Both of us change and then I climb into my bed, before TJ gets in right behind me. My chest still aches. I still can't stop thinking about the day, but as TJ throws a leg over me, and buries his face in my chest, I realize I've never felt so settled in my own skin either.

Chapter 25

"WILL YOU check that text on my phone?" I ask TJ as I drive his SUV toward New York.

He grabs my cell from the cup holder and looks at it. "It's your mom. She said she's worried about you because you were so upset yesterday. She wants to know if you're feeling better."

Oh. Well, that's embarrassing. I shrug. "I was kind of trippin' out when I called her. All that stuff with Greg. She worries."

TJ sets my phone down, and puts his hand on the back of my neck. "Your face is red. Why is that embarrassing to you? That's what parents do. Mine was the same way when I talked to her."

"I'm not embarrassed."

"Oh, you're a liar. We've been together for a day, and you're already lying to me. It's like I can't even trust you!" TJ jerks his hand away, crosses his arms and looks out the window. I can see his smile in the reflection.

"It won't happen again! I'm sorry," I say, playing along with him.

TJ whips his head in my direction. "Then you're forgiven." He winks, and then his hand is at the back of my neck again. It's crazy how I always have so much fun with him. Even something that shouldn't be such a good time, is.

It doesn't take long for us to get to New York. The city is crazy to drive in, with all sorts of lanes full of standstill traffic, people honking at each other and letting people out in the middle of the street. I'm really wishing I would've made him drive it instead of me. All I need is to wreck his car. My mom will lose it.

We survive and get to the hotel. "We'll take a cab wherever we go. Parking is crazy and costs a ton. At least if we leave the car here we only have to pay at the hotel," he tells me as we make our way to the room.

"What's the plan while we're here?" I ask him.

"It's a secret, remember? Stop trying to get stuff out of me. I won't budge." TJ nudges my arm. "Oh, here's our room." Which is tiny. It's the smallest of the rooms we've stayed in, and I'm betting the most expensive.

We go inside, and TJ immediately jumps onto his computer and starts screwing around with video. I sit with him for a while, but there's only so long I can do it. I'm just not as into it as he is and after a couple hours, I move to the bed and watch some TV. Before I know it, TJ's hand is on my shoulder and he's waking me up.

"Oh, shit. How long have I been out?" I ask him.

"Not long. Go back to bed. I'm going to run get us something to eat and meet someone real quick. I'll be right back."

I try to get up, but he shakes his head.

"Stay. It'll only take like half an hour or something. Go back to sleep. You were snoring like crazy." He laughs but then bends down and kisses me quickly. "Be right back."

Of course I'm now totally awake. As I sit up, my cell goes off with Chase's ringer. *Shit.* I haven't talked to him since I left. I almost ignore it but then click talk. No matter what, he's my best friend. He always has been, and he always will be. Chase may give me hell, but I also know he'd knock someone out if they ever did. He's loyal like that. He just has a big mouth too.

"What's up?" I ask him.

"What's up? What's up? What the fuck, Collins? You're the one who got out of town for spring break, left our asses here, and then dropped off the face of the earth. How about you tell us what's up so we can live vicariously through you."

Marcus and Jabbar yell something in the background, but I can't make it out.

It's on the tip of my tongue to lie. To make up some lame story about what I'm doing with my uncle, but I'm so tired of that. I don't want to keep making the same mistakes. I don't want to have regrets. I want to know my friends are totally okay with who I am. "Dude, it's been awesome. I'm um… I'm not with my uncle. I'm with TJ. We're on this road trip because he's—"

"Who's TJ? Do we know a TJ?" When he asks if they know a TJ, I think he's directing it toward Marcus and Jabbar.

After standing up, I start pacing the room because pacing is totally going to make this easier. Yeah right. "The guy from The Spot, remember? You guys saw him in there a few times. He's the one who—"

"The one you pretended not to know before you pushed me in the parking lot?" Chase's voice is calm, but for him, calm means pissed. "Why did you say you were with your uncle? And you're on a fucking road trip and didn't tell us? What the hell, man?"

"Why didn't I tell you? Come on, like you would've really wanted to know." *Because seeing me with a guy will be weird.* "It's not a big a deal. I just... he's doing this really cool documentary thing, and I wanted to go. It was important for me to go and—"

"But it was also important for you to lie to us about it, obviously. That's awesome, Collins. We've had your back no matter what. It's not like we don't know... about you. That was a dick thing to do. It's not like we'd care."

It's not like they don't know I'm gay. He can't even use the word. But then, it's not like I've ever really talked to him about it either. I told him once and then avoided the conversation of me and guys at all costs. "It's not—"

"Someone's on the other line. We're out. Have fun on your road trip." Then there's nothing but silence.

Squeezing my phone, I almost throw it across the room but stop myself. The last thing I need to do is break my cell, but dude, what's his problem? It's not like I have to tell him what I do at all times. It's not like he really wants to hear about me with another guy or having a boyfriend anyway.

After putting my phone on the charger, I grab my bag and head into the bathroom. My shower is quick, and then I wrap a towel around my waist as I brush my teeth. Seriously, does Chase not realize how big a deal this is? I told him the truth. I admitted where I am, and that wasn't easy.

The door clicks. Toothbrush hanging out of my mouth, I turn toward it just as TJ walks in rubbing his hands together. "Shit. It's cold out there." His gaze scans the room before landing on me in the bathroom. "What's wrong?"

How does he know something's wrong?

As I spit and rinse my mouth out, TJ comes into the bathroom, closes the toilet lid, and sits down. It's then I realize I don't have anything on except for a towel, with a guy who is my boyfriend. A guy who I see as someone other than a friend. It's another thing that I've only had with him.

"You're embarrassed again, Bradley. It's so strange. Only your neck and part of your face turns red. Not the whole thing. You have like, selective blushing, or something."

What the? "Selective blushing?"

"What would you call it? And do you want me to leave? You looked pissed when I first came in. You're really transparent, by the way. You should work on that."

Sometimes he talks so much and says the most random things, I'm not sure how to reply to him. But I like that about him. "I should?"

"Or not." He shakes his head. "Definitely not. I like to know what's going on with you. So what happened?"

Before I know it, I'm leaning against the bathroom counter, and I've spilled the whole story out for him.

TJ's eyebrows pull together. "You told him you were with your uncle?"

Shit. I didn't even think of that when I was telling him the story. "Yes. But are you really surprised? I told him now. I didn't have to do it, but I told him now." He nods, but I can tell he's disappointed. "I'm sorry."

TJ waves his hand. "It's okay. I don't know why I didn't expect it. But you're right, you told him. That's what matters. I'm sorry he's pissed but maybe that makes what I'm about to tell you even better."

"What?" I ask.

TJ stands up, walks over, and stops right in front of me. He stands with his legs spread a little, so mine are between his, like we were against the wall of the hotel yesterday. "I have a surprise for you. I know we've both been bummed since yesterday, and I figured we could use something fun. But that's only a partial truth because I've obviously had this planned for a while."

My pulse starts going crazy. "Had what planned? Spit it out."

He touches my waist with his left hand, his thumb brushing over my oblique muscles. It makes me shiver and wish for more. He pushes his right hand in his pocket, pulls something out, and holds it up to me. An ID with my picture. The one he took when we were in the restaurant, though it's obviously been altered. Even if it wasn't on a New York license.

"For tonight, you're twenty-one, Mr. Michael Jordan. We're going to a gay club."

Chapter 26

"MICHAEL JORDAN? You couldn't have thought of another name besides the most popular basketball player of all time?" I ask TJ as we walk down the busy street. It's dark out, about nine something. We just got out of a cab, down the street from the club we're going to. Not sure why we're walking part of the way but I'm glad. Maybe he needs the time to chill as much as I do.

"You like basketball. It's not really my thing. It was that or LeBron James. I couldn't think of anyone else."

I squeeze his hand that I'm holding in mine. "Tell me you're joking."

"I'm joking." He laughs.

He's totally not joking. "Who are you?"

"Martin—"

My feet stick to the pavement, and he stops walking too. "Martin? You could have made up a name like that for me."

"I didn't make it up, sports guy. You didn't let me finish. Martin Scorsese."

I drop my head backward and look at the sky. Foggy plums of my breath float up. "And you don't think the bouncer will notice when an ex-professional basketball player and the dude who directs all of Leonardo DiCaprio's movies comes to the club?"

"*Goodfellas*. He directed *Goodfellas*. And it'll be fine. I promise they don't really give a shit. All they care about is that the ID says we're twenty-one. Don't worry." He grabs my face and tilts it down so I'm looking at him. "Go to a gay club with me, Bradley. I've never been. I want...." He shrugs. "I want us to have a good time. I want you to see it's okay. That there are millions of people like us. They're happy and healthy and that it's okay. That it's better than okay."

The glow from the streetlight above makes it easier for me to see him.

"I know we're talking to different people here and there but not all of it is happy. And it's limited. It's just...." TJ looks down, almost as if he's unsure.

For the first time since I've known him, TJ doesn't finish a sentence. I realize then what he's thinking. That when we go back, I'll freak out. That I won't want to be with him anymore. That I think there's something wrong with who we are. That's never been it. I've never believed that, but I'm not sure I gave him any reason to think otherwise either. Or maybe he's right, and I'm just lying to myself. "I'll go. But I know it's okay to be gay too." Even though I said no to Mom each time she wanted me to talk to someone or go to the LGBT group. Even though I avoided going out with someone, and acted like an idiot when he approached me back home. Do I? Do I really know it's okay?

"I know it's stupid, using a club as an example. That's not reality, but it'll be fun. We'll see so many people who, no matter how different they are, they're just like us in that one way."

And I want that. Want to go with him. Want to go do this, and to have fun with TJ. "Let's do it, Martin." I nod my head toward the club.

TJ smiles, and it's a different kind of smile than I've ever seen from him. Unsure, but happy. "Lead the way, Michael."

My heart slams against my rib cage, basketball to court floor over and over as the bouncer looks at my ID. He has pink hair and arms as big as my head—oh, that I can totally see because he's wearing a T-shirt even though it's freezing balls outside.

He holds the ID back out for me, and I try and calm my shaking hands when I reach for it, but he pulls it back a little right before I can grab it. *Oh shit.* TJ's grip tightens on my other hand.

"I forgot, I need to mark you first." Big arms grins, but I'm thinking *mark me?* What the heck does that mean?

Then he picks up a marker. Grabs my hand and makes a circle on it, before giving me the ID and finally enabling me to breathe.

"Next," he says, and I step out of the way for TJ's turn. Maybe I shouldn't admit this, maybe it shouldn't be true, but that was exciting.

The ID inspection goes much quicker with TJ, and then we're walking down a long, dark hallway getting closer and closer to the wild thump of music. It reminds me of the party with Richie and Dave except when we go through the doors, I'm figuring I'll have to times it by a hundred—more people, louder music, more space, more alcohol. More everything.

Oh, and TJ and I won't be the only guys together the way Richie and Dave were.

There are black double doors in front of us. The line of people behind us are all shouting and pulsing with energy, ready to get inside. So, I push the door open and realize my assessment was completely wrong. This is the party times a thousand, and—"Is that a slide?" I yell at TJ.

He steps inside, mouth to my ear and says, "That is definitely a slide. In the middle of the room."

That is badass.

Chapter 27

PEOPLE SHOVE their way around us, so TJ and I back out of the way. We both scan the massive room stuffed with people. There is a bar on each of the four walls. People are dancing, men are kissing men, and women are kissing women. Others are talking and others are alone. People are *sliding,* and drinking, and we totally shouldn't be in here right now, but I'm so stoked that we are.

"Do you wanna get a drink?" I ask because we're twenty-one now, and I feel like that means we should.

"I'm okay if you are. Either way!" TJ's still close.

"I'm good right now." There's too much excitement, too much *everything* around us. Those are the things I want to experience.

"Same here. Slide with me, sports guy." And then he's pulling me along, our hands still clasped together. I'm laughing, though I'm not sure why. Still, I think TJ might be laughing with me. We find the end of the line and grab spots. Two girls are in front of us, bouncing and clinging to each other.

"Have you done this before? It's so awesome!" The girl with the long hair says to us.

"No. This is our first time," TJ replies to her.

"I'm Amy! This is Lisa!"

"TJ and Bradley. We're new to New York!" They're shouting back and forth because that's the only way to hear each other over the music.

This time it's Lisa who speaks. "You guys will love it! You came to the perfect place for a good time!"

The line moves up, and so do we. We learn that Amy and Lisa are seniors at NYU. They've been together for a year, both of them very out and proud. Both of them with supportive families and they're part of a LGBT group that works to spread positivity in the community and resources. They run the chapter at NYU.

"That's incredible. Bradley and I are making a documentary about gay life and history."

It's awesome that he includes me as though this is something we came up with together, as if it's something we're on equal footing on when we both know we're not. This is all him. I'm just lucky he's taking me along for the ride.

It's that that makes me lean over. Makes me kiss him on the cheek. He's my boyfriend, and I'm proud of that. I want him to know it, and to know how much I appreciate what we're doing.

TJ turns to look at me and winks.

We're on the stairs by now, about half of the way up. I'm figuring they went with stairs as it's harder to fall down them than a ladder.

"That sounds cool," Amy tells us, but I'm still looking at TJ. He said before it was annoying how much he liked me. I realize now that I feel the same about him. I like him more than I ever would have thought.

"Oh, you got it bad. You guys are totally cute." Amy ruffles my hair like I'm twelve. "Is he your first boyfriend? But not your first, right, TJ?"

"Dude." I snap my attention her way. "How do you know?" Do I radiate my virgin-boyfriend status or something? And wait. How does she know I'm not TJ's first? Does that mean I look more into him than he is me?

"It's not a bad thing. It's sweet. You just look at him like you're in awe of him. Like you can't believe you're here with him."

Hopefully that's a drunk-girl assessment. Not that I don't look at him and can't believe I'm with him, because I do. But I want....

"I'm in awe of him too." TJ goes up the stairs, sort of dragging me along with him, like he didn't just say what he did. There's no reason to be in awe of me. We both know that. I'm not always nice. I don't always do the right thing, but when he says it, I believe him. TJ's not the type of guy to lie, and I want to be the kind of guy he should be in awe of. Not just for him but for me.

"First love is so cute!" Lisa shouts. Amy pulls something out of the purse she has around her.

"Here's my number. Call us if you need any help with your documentary," Amy tells TJ, and then it's their turn, and they're twisting and turning their way down the slide. All I can think about is TJ being in awe of me. Not because I kick ass on the court or because I'm popular or any other reasons except the fact that I'm me, and he seems to like that person.

"Wanna go down together?" I ask him.

"What kind of question is that?" TJ grins and sits down. I sit behind him, wrap my arms and legs around TJ, and then we push off. The music blasts around us, and people below us are dancing and laughing. Air whips around us, and I squeeze him tighter. Me—Bradley Collins. The only openly gay guy at my school, going down a slide in a gay bar in New York with my boyfriend, and thinking that's a pretty amazing person to be.

I GO to every dance at my school. Everyone does. It's the thing to do. Sometimes the guys go with a date, sometimes they don't, but I'm always there with them. And I dance. Dance with girls we're friends with. Dance with girls who used to think I liked them before I came out, and afterward who knew I was gay, yet I was Bradley Collins. The point guard. Best friend of Chase, Marcus, and Jabbar. The guy who made prom court my sophomore year.

Tonight I'm dancing at a club in New York with my boyfriend. Like so many things, this is a first for me. The first time I've danced with any guy, not just one who has a title.

We go down the slide again before TJ asks if I want to dance. We squeeze between the hundreds of other people moving together on the dance floor, and then do the same as them. TJ and I, our bodies matching, moving with each other. I'm sweating—we dance forever, but I don't want to stop either. There's that buzz under my skin again that only TJ gives me, and I want it to last, want to feel this high I get by being me.

We haven't had a drink all night. We could have gone to an eighteen and older club, but I'm not sure drinking was the reason we came here. Maybe it was the excitement of doing something against the rules, or maybe TJ thought it would distract me from other things, or maybe I'm totally going out on a crazy limb here and it was because we were somehow *supposed* to meet Amy and Lisa. Who knows if that was anything important, but it feels like it. Everything on this trip has felt important.

We stay at the club until a little after one. This won't be part of the documentary. We both knew that going into it. Tonight was just for us.

"Did you have fun?" TJ asks as we ride in the back of a cab.

"I won't change my mind. When we get back, I mean. Things won't change."

TJ takes a minute to respond. "You might not think they will, but that doesn't mean they won't. The things with your friends that were hard and awkward are still going to be hard and awkward when you see them again."

Before this trip, I never would have had a boyfriend right now. I would have been embarrassed to. Not anymore. "I'll prove you wrong."

The cabbie pulls up in front of our hotel. TJ pays him without another word.

Chapter 28

WHEN WE get into the room, I go straight to the bathroom to take a leak. Afterward I wash my hands, brush my teeth, and then go back into the other room. TJ is waiting outside the door in his boxers and a T-shirt.

"Stop staring and get out of the way. I gotta piss." He has the light, teasing sound back in his voice.

I step back. "I wasn't staring."

"Yes you were. You're in *awe* of me, remember?"

"Hey! I never said I was in awe of you. Amy did. You're the one who said you're in awe of me." Yeah. *What now, TJ?*

He shrugs. "I never denied it." Then he closes himself inside the bathroom, and I'm standing outside like an idiot. He is way too good at this. I want to be good at it too. I'm always the one who gets knocked for a loop with TJ.

Before he comes out, I take off my jeans, change my shirt and get into bed in my boxers. I hear water running, and TJ's in there for another minute or so before he opens the bathroom door and turns out the light. He hits the light beside my bed next. There's no movement, and I think he's going to get into the other bed, but then mine dips and he's under the blankets next to me.

All sorts of words play through my head. Things I want to tell him or ask him. Things I probably *should* tell him, but I figure he's a guy. He'll get the fact that words are way harder than action.

Instead of opening my mouth to speak, I roll to my right side and face him. I put my hand on his waist and pull so he rolls over too. We're looking at each other in the dark, though we really can't see each other all that well.

"Hi," he says.

"Hey." It's almost like I'm watching my movements. As though I'm outside of my body. Watching my arm lift. Watching my hand touch his hair. It feels like he brushed the gel out, so it's not spiked like he wears it during the day.

Pushing up on my right elbow, I look down at his shape in the dark. Watch myself lean forward. Now, I'm in my body again. I feel his lips against mine. Feel the little bit of growth on his face that he'll shave away in the morning. Feel his mouth loosen up. Feel it open. Feel his tongue against my tongue. Taste his toothpaste and wonder if he tastes mine.

I let my hand slide down and move to his waist again. His shirt has lifted up so it's skin-on-skin. His body feels warm, and I'm thankful it's not just me. Mine is on fire.

My hand moves to his abs, feeling muscle under hot skin. TJ deepens the kiss, his arm going around my neck and pulling me closer. The flames inside me ignite hotter and hotter. My body wants it all, but my head and nerves keep pushing their way in.

It makes me pull back slightly. TJ kisses me again, this time it's his lips pressing to mine. He rolls me to my back, going with me so he lies on top of me. It's obvious his body wants exactly what mine does. The proof is against me. We're in a hotel, alone, hundreds of miles from our parents, and I want this, I really do, but the fear digs its claws into me deeper. What if I don't know what to do? What if it sucks? What if *I* suck? What if he wants to do it to me?

My hormones are screaming at me, *you're an eighteen-year-old guy. You don't give a shit about this stuff!* But then the questions slam into me again like they're on repeat. *What if I don't know what to do? What if it sucks? What if I suck? What if he wants to do it to me?*

I don't even know if I'm supposed to worry about that last one, but I do.

TJ seems to know because he stops kissing, pushes my hair off my forehead and says, "What's wrong, sports guy?"

My hormones kick in yelling, *Nothing! Nothing is wrong!* "I don't... don't know if we should...."

I expect him to pull away, but instead he chuckles and then buries his face in my neck. "I wasn't going to try and have sex with you. I mean, unless you want to have sex. Then I totally will, but I wasn't going to try. Not yet."

He doesn't move, his hips resting between my legs. I know he feels that my body wants this just as much as his obviously wants me, but he doesn't mention it.

"Have you ever had sex with a guy?" I ask.

"Well I definitely haven't had it with a girl."

"You're funny, film boy. Maybe you should consider being a comedian instead. That's not what I meant."

He pulls his face out of my neck. "Sorry. Yes, I've had sex."

The fire inside me suddenly transforms into something else. Jealousy. I'm jealous because he's done everything I haven't. I'm jealous that he liked someone enough, or at least wanted them enough to be with them. It brings me back to that line at the slide when the girls said I look at him differently than he looks at me.

"With how many people?"

"Actual sex, sex? Just one. But I've done other stuff with a couple other guys. That doesn't mean I'm some sex-fiend, though. It's not a big deal for me to wait, Bradley. I...." He pushes my hair back again. "It's different with you, yeah? That sounds cheesy, but it's true." He rolls off me but doesn't pull away. His head rests in the crook of my arm, his hand under my shirt.

And I'm suddenly not jealous anymore. My body is telling me I'm really, really stupid again for making him hit the brakes.

"Did you... damn, this is embarrassing. Never mind." I try to roll away, but he doesn't let me.

"Don't be embarrassed. I didn't receive if that's what you're asking. But I will if that's what you want. If you ever want, I mean."

"I want now." I laugh. "That's not the problem. It's just...." The idea is scary as hell. None of my friends are virgins, and I don't want to be either, but I don't think I can go there yet.

"It's okay. I get it. At least I didn't get slammed in the head with a door when sex came up this time."

"It's different with you too," I tell him.

Softly, he replies, "I'm your first boyfriend."

"So?" And then we're both quiet while I wrack my brain to think of something to say. A change in conversation is pretty much a must at this point. "Do you ever go by Thomas? Do your parents call you that or does everyone call you TJ?"

"When I was fourteen I told my parents I wanted to be called TJ. No one has called me Thomas since then."

"Why?"

"It's easier? Why else? My dad and I always answered at the wrong time when people called me Thomas."

"Your parents just went with it?" I ask.

"Are we really going to go from talking about sex to my parents? That weirds me out." TJ gets close to me, mumbling into my chest as he speaks. "I'm tired. Let's go to sleep. We can talk parents when I don't have a boner."

Like always, he makes me laugh. "Yeah, I can agree with that one. But... I mean, just because we aren't going to have sex, doesn't mean there's not other things we can do." Even though I'm not sure about going all the way, I want something. Want to feel him and have him feel me and know what it's like to be with someone like that.

"We don't have to. I know this is new... and yeah, *we're* new too."

"You don't want to?"

"Are you kidding me? Of course, I want to. It's just... I don't wanna feel like I'm taking advantage of the situation. I want you to really want it."

Because there's any possibility I don't? Not likely. "I do. We can...." I don't know what to suggest. I also don't get his hesitation.

"Here," TJ whispers softly. "Let me." And then his hand drifts down, under the waistband of my boxers. As soon as he touches me, I hiss and TJ starts pulling his hand back.

"No. Don't," I manage to say.

"You sure?" he asks again.

"Totally stupid question."

He doesn't laugh, but his hand goes down again, wraps around me like I've done to myself a million times. Only it's different with him, and it ends quicker than it usually does. I'm pretty sure it's the most incredible thing that's ever happened to me, though. My breathing is hard, but I manage to say, "Holy shit... um... yeah. Want me to...?"

TJ pauses. Waits. His voice is soft when he says, "No. It's okay. Let's just go to sleep."

Disappointment bounces around inside me. He made me feel good, and I want to return the favor. Still, I get out of bed and clean up before climbing back in. TJ wraps an arm around me. "You're okay with it...?" Soft breath hits my neck. Sometimes in moments like these, it feels like things are as new to TJ as they are to me. Suddenly I'm not disappointed anymore.

"I'm more than okay with it. I'm stoked to do it again." His shirt was right. It definitely felt like special effects to me.

He laughs but still doesn't offer himself to me. "Night, sports guy."

Closing my eyes, I smile. "Night, film boy." And then we both go to sleep.

Chapter 29

THE NEXT morning TJ is in his zone again as he gets everything ready for our interview. When we're in the cab, he stares out the window, watching buildings go by like it's any other day.

He seems to have completely forgotten about last night, but it hasn't left my head at all yet. I got a hand job. A hand job from someone other than myself. Sex is pretty much always on my mind, but now it's going overtime. It makes me get why Chase, Jabbar, and Marcus talk or think about girls anytime we're not playing ball. Now I have someone that I could eventually have sex with, and though there's way more to TJ than that, it's a pretty exciting piece of it.

"Twenty-five sixty," the cabbie tells us, making me realize we stopped. We're in front of a huge apartment building downtown. It's got this older look to it, but I think that's on purpose. I have no doubt that whatever is inside, is nice.

"I got it," I tell TJ as I pull my wallet out of my pocket.

"Thanks." TJ starts shoving his papers into his bag as the cabbie looks at us like we're wasting his day. After paying him, I help TJ get the equipment out of the car, and then we're waiting for the doorman to let us in.

"This is cool. I feel like I'm in a TV show or something." We don't have doormen like this at home.

"I forget you've never been to any of the states we've gone. I was born in New York. I wish we had more time. Maybe we can come back this summer, or something." The words are steady, automatic, as though he expects us to still be together months from now. I want us to be. I'm stunned at the awesomeness of it. When I manage to snap myself out of it, I have to jog to catch up with him.

"That'd be cool. We should definitely do it."

TJ nods, and then we're let inside. It doesn't take long for the elevator to take us up to the eighteenth floor. Before I know it, we're standing at a door and a black woman is opening it.

"Hey, guys. I'm so glad you could make it." Her voice is a little high-pitched, like it's floating on happy. She steps aside for us. Waiting, I let TJ go in first before I step in behind him.

"Hi. Michelle, this is Bradley, Bradley this is Michelle."

I reach out, and shake her hand. "Hey. Nice to meet you."

"You as well. We can head into the living room, guys. Just keep going straight." Michelle is tall, wearing a long-sleeved, button-up shirt and one of those long, tight skirts like she's been at work or something. Who knows, maybe that's just how she dresses.

The living room is spotless. Nothing out of place, but to the far right is a smaller room attached that's full of toys. When I say full, I mean, is-there-space-to-walk full.

"Is Layla here?" TJ asks her.

"No. She'll be here soon, though. Set up whatever you need. We can move furniture around if it helps."

I have no clue who Layla is but don't ask.

TJ eyes the room, stopping on a built-in bookcase on one of the walls. "It'll work. Can I see that bag, Bradley?"

I hand it over to him, and then the two of us start getting unpacked. We position the tripod by the bookcase before plugging equipment in. It's second nature by now, and I can do it all without any instruction from TJ.

The setup goes quickly. Michelle grabs both of us a bottle of water, and then we're sitting down, camera on, Michelle in front of it, and TJ and me off to the side.

"Can I ask what you do for a living?" TJ says to her.

"No."

My eyes go wide, and TJ's head snaps in Michelle's direction, but then she chuckles. "I'm kidding. Of course. I'm a cardiologist."

Whoa. A heart doctor.

"Married?" TJ questions. I'm sure I won't be saying anything for a while considering I don't even know why we're here yet.

"No."

"In a relationship?" TJ writes something down.

"Yes. We've been together for ten years. Stacy is a doctor as well. We have plans to get married."

"I see a room full of toys across from us. Do you have kids?"

"We do." Michelle smiles. "She's six. She's been with us since she was two."

Hmm. So this is about having a kid? "You adopted her?" I ask, and then realize it was a stupid question. How else would she have gotten a two-year-old?

"I did. My partner and I always wanted children. It was one of the first questions she asked me on our first date. The goal has been a part of us from the very beginning. It wasn't an easy road, but when you want something bad enough, you don't give up on it. We didn't."

My mom said all she ever wanted to be was a mom. She's a nurse and she loves it, but she said she could be happy just having kids. She always tells me how stoked she was when she found out she was pregnant with me. And Dad was too, according to her, but I've always wondered if that was true. I remember hearing a fight between them not long before Dad bailed. He accused her of trying to trap him. He said she knew he wasn't happy but had then gotten pregnant with my brother on purpose so he couldn't leave.

First, having kids obviously didn't matter because once he did leave, he never came back. And second, I think my mom is probably the most honorable person I know. If he thought that about her, he never knew her. Plus, I'm pretty sure it takes two people for a girl to get pregnant.

The smile on Michelle's face at the mention of their child tells me their daughter will probably never have to wonder if her parents wanted her or how much they want to raise her. At least not from Michelle. Something tells me Stacy is probably the same, though.

"You said it wasn't an easy road," TJ says. "Can you tell us how so?"

Michelle wrings her hands together. "Because we're gay women, in demanding careers who want to have a child."

"The state made it difficult?"

"In a way yes, but even our families at first. Both Stacy and I came out later in life. It's hard when you're young. I was scared, and she just didn't want it to be true. We both came out in our thirties, right before we met. Our families were still getting used to us being lesbians when we got together, and we got serious quickly."

"What did your families do when you told them you were thinking of adopting?" TJ asks her.

"They tried to talk us out of it—all of them. Had we thought this through? Doesn't a child deserve a mom and a dad? Did we really want to put a child through that?"

Leaning forward, I ask, "Through what?" Having two parents who want her? Who love her?

"Through the absolute horror of having two gay parents who love each other, who would do anything for a child, of course," she says with a mocking grin. She gets serious again when she adds, "They were worried about how people would react. People get strange ideas in their head, but we didn't think that was our problem."

"Did they worry about the kid?" TJ writes on his notepad as he speaks.

"They did. They worried about when Layla started school. If people would tease her or if she would suffer for it. Stacy and I never stopped thinking about what she might face. The last thing either of us wanted was to set a child up to have problems. Stacy had been bullied as a child, for different reasons, and the thought of a child of ours going through that because of us, kept Stacy and I up many nights. People were worried that being raised by gay parents would make her confused about her sexuality—especially since we knew we wanted a girl. That's not something we worried about as much, but it was another thing in the back of our minds."

Michelle pauses, twisting a ring on her finger, before glancing at the camera, and then us. "As a woman... someone telling me that I wouldn't make a good mom? That Stacy and I wouldn't make good parents together? That was the hardest part. A lot of women, that's what we want more than anything—to be a mom. We are smart, capable people yet the individuals in our life who were supposed to love us the most, wanted to take away this basic human right of ours. I'm not going to say it wasn't a blow to both of us. And yes, there were other options. One of us could carry a child, but there are so many babies that need homes out there, and we wanted to help one of them."

"What made you decide to go for it?" TJ looks at me though he's surprised by my question.

"Stop reading my mind." He grins, and I like the fact that I would ask something he wanted to know.

"We remembered that there wasn't a damn thing wrong with our love. That our relationship is just as real, and deserves the same kind of happiness as anyone else's. We remembered why we wanted to adopt in the first place. We loved each other. We wanted to share that love with a child who needed it. And then we remembered that if anyone gave her a hard time, she'd have two moms to stick up for her. You haven't seen anything until you've seen a mom protecting her child." Michelle smiles.

"In all honesty, though. We wanted to love a child. We wanted to give her a home. A good *home*, where she would belong and not have to worry about going from place to place. What's wrong with that?"

Nothing.

"So you decided to go for it, regardless of what your families thought?" TJ adds.

"Yes, but I have to say they came around fairly quickly. We saw Layla not long after she was born, and we knew she was the one. My mom saw her once and knew it as well. It took a while to get everyone else on the same page. She has a couple learning delays and a few medical problems she was born with. We had extra hoops to jump through, but we did it. We did it because we love her. It took two years, but she's ours."

"And now?" TJ asks.

"And now she runs our house." Michelle laughs. "She's happy. She's loved. She developed more quickly than they expected. She's sharp. Sometimes I wonder if she's smarter than me. But again, the most important thing is, she's happy."

Just then, there's a noise behind us. I turn just as the door opens and another woman comes in. As soon as she does, a little girl with braids in her hair runs toward the living room. "Mommy! Mommy!"

Michelle "umpfs" as the kid launches herself at her.

"We can edit her out if you want. I wasn't sure if you wanted her on camera or not," TJ tells her.

"She's part of the family. It's okay."

Stacy introduces herself, pushes her blond hair behind her ears, and then sits on the couch with Layla and Michelle. The little girl climbs all over them both, laughing the whole time.

"Who are you?" Layla asks us.

Glancing at TJ, I wait for him to answer. "We're friends of your moms."

"Mommy or Mama?" She crosses her arms.

"Both," I reply.

"Why's there a camera?" is her next question. That's another one I let TJ handle.

"We're talking to them about how happy they are that you're their daughter." He grins at her, at ease like always.

She gets the biggest smile on her face and lifts her shoulders as though the happiness is trying to take her over. "I'm happy too. I love my moms."

It's the perfect end to our interview. We finish with her bouncing around her moms, who give her more attention than the camera.

We stay for about an hour after the interview is done. Layla drags TJ and me into her playroom. I don't know anything about little girls, and I'm kind of uncomfortable at first, but it's pretty obvious that Michelle was right. She runs the show.

The whole time all I can do is watch Layla. I think she might be the happiest kid on the planet.

When we go to leave, Michelle stops us right before we walk out the door. "If there's one thing I want you to take from this it's to never let anyone tell you you can't do something, or you shouldn't do something because of who you love. You deserve whatever you want, as long as you're willing to fight for it."

Chapter 30

WE'RE WALKING through Central Park, which doesn't look nearly as cool as it does on TV. TJ says it's better in the summer and fall, which makes sense. The trees are bare right now and everything is gray. I'm still glad we came, though. I can't come to NYC and not go to Central Park. It's cool to see what's practically a forest in the middle of a city.

"Are your parents happy, film boy?" I avoid stepping on cracks as we make our way down the sidewalk.

"You're way too obsessed with my parents."

"Ha-ha."

"Hold my hand and I'll tell you." He nudges me.

"You don't have to bribe me." I latch our fingers together.

"Yeah, they're happy. They're totally in love. They've been together since he was seventeen and Mom was sixteen. He came from money, she didn't. She would do anything to make him happy, and he loves her for it."

"That's cool."

"Until you see them kiss. Then it's not cool," he teases.

There's this idea swimming around in my head, an idea that's been around longer than I'd like to admit. There's a part of me who wants to let it out. Who wants TJ to tell me it's wrong, but then I really don't want him to know I've been thinking it either. It makes this emptiness sort of spread through me, opening up more space inside me for guilt. It's wrong. I shouldn't think it, but then I guess we can't always control those things.

"Where's your head at? You get this spaced-out look in your eyes when you're thinking about or stressing about something."

I glance at him. "I do?" No one's ever said that to me before.

"You do. It's cute, but it's not always followed by something good, so then I get too freaked to enjoy it."

Trying to keep my facial expression serious, I say, "You should never be too *anything* to enjoy my good looks."

"Funny guy." When he nudges me this time, I step away, but then TJ pulls me right back again.

"I'm embarrassed to say." That's not something I would have said to anyone else. It's something small but not something I'm proud of either. I don't want to be too embarrassed to do or say anything. Not acknowledging it makes it easier to pretend it's not true. But if there's anyone who won't judge me for it, it's TJ.

"We're all embarrassed by something. We all have secrets, Bradley."

"Not you."

"If you say so." He pauses and then says, "Tell me. I'll even say please."

"Then say it." I stall.

"I just did." He rolls his eyes but then adds, "Please." He stops walking and stands in front of me. "I wanna know everything about you."

Holy shit. He is way, way, way too good at this. But it's genuine. Everything about him is.

"I sometimes wonder…." I shrug. "That if my dad hadn't left… if I would have had him around instead of just Mom… if he would have *really* been there, when he was there, if I wouldn't be gay." My breath gets trapped in my throat as I wait for TJ to reply. His eyes wrinkle around the corners.

"I mean, I know in my head that can't be true. I do but…. He never did much with us. It was always her. That's dumb. I can't believe I just said that." I try to pull my hand away, but TJ holds on.

"You're gay because you were born gay. No one can change it, no matter how much they want to. Who you're raised with doesn't matter." He almost looks disappointed. He bites his bottom lip, then lets out a deep breath. "We are who we are."

"I know. I don't know why I've questioned that sometimes."

"The real question is, if that were true, would you want to change it? Not because you miss your dad but because you don't want to be gay?"

Tilting my head down, I look at our hands. At our fingers threaded together. I concentrate on how it feels. How he feels. How he makes me feel not just when we're touching but all the time. And then I think about myself too. The things TJ and I have done on this trip. What this documentary could someday do. The kind of friend I am most of the time and the kind of son and brother I am. I'm a good guy. There's nothing wrong with me. And I like being with him.

"No. I wouldn't change it. You make me get way sappier than any guy should ever get."

TJ's smile changes his whole face. It's happy again. Light. "That's because I'm hot. And I can kiss. You can't help but love me."

He's right. He's definitely hot. He can definitely kiss. I don't really know what it feels like to be in love with someone, but I can't imagine it feeling much better than this.

"Hey, get your camera," I tell him. TJ pulls it out of his pocket and I take it from him. Holding it at arm's length, I turn it backward. TJ leans in close, his cheek to mine, and I push the button.

THE NEXT day, a cab drops us off in front of Rainbow Warriors. Amy stands in the window, waving her arm back and forth as though we somehow missed the place or something. TJ'd called her when we got back to the room last night, and she said we could come down today. He brought his camera with him so he can get a little on film about what they do here.

As soon as we step inside, Amy hugs him and Lisa does the same to me before they switch. Amy has her long, fair hair tied up. Lisa's is purple, something I didn't notice in the dark club.

"We're so glad you guys could come," Lisa says.

"Thanks. We're glad to be here," TJ replies.

There's a woman sitting behind a desk answering the phone. All around the room are pictures from events. I walk around to look at all of them, and soon TJ's joining me, recording it all with his camera. They have pictures from pride parades, marches, and protests. They have events where they feed the homeless, and fund-raisers, and all sorts of other things.

"Right now our focus is on youth on the streets. Did you know that over 40 percent of the homeless youth are gay? Most of them running away either because of fear of coming out, or parents kicking them out when they find out they are gay?" Amy crosses her arms.

Forty percent. Holy shit. That's a lot. I think about Dustin/Shaun, and Matt, and Henry, and other people who are in the closet or had a hard time coming out. That could have been them. I don't know Matt's history. Maybe it was him.

"What do you guys do for them?" I ask her.

"We coordinate with shelters in the area. There are some who specialize in LGBT youth. We help with whatever they need and also provide food, take clothes donations and things like that. We also have hotlines—some for homeless and others for at risk youth. Those who might consider suicide. We have a few counselors here but not enough. That's what Lisa is going to school for." She points to her girlfriend.

"We're sorry we don't have much time. We're actually heading out for one of the food drives right now." Amy takes her purse from Lisa.

"Can we go?" sort of tumbles out of my mouth.

"Want to?" Lisa asks.

"Absolutely." This from TJ.

Then the four of us are climbing into another cab, and we're riding across town to do something that matters. My body feels all jittery, full of life. I look over at TJ. It's because of him that I'm here. Because of him that I realize I'm okay with being me. Because of him that I'm finally starting to live with my eyes open the way I told him I wanted to do.

Chapter 31

WE'VE BEEN here for three hours. We've given out food and each time I pass a plate to someone, I wonder if Greg and Darren felt this... fulfilled when they did stuff like this. Greg said Darren used to like to volunteer, that he would do it for Darren, and I think maybe he did it for himself too.

I'm sitting at one of the tables, taking a short break when a girl sits down across from me. Two weeks ago I wouldn't have said a word to her, but I'm not sure that's possible now. "Hey," I say. "My name's Bradley. What's yours?"

"Tammy." She twists the strings on her worn-out hoodie. She glances down as though she doesn't want to make eye contact with me. Then she starts playing with the zipper, and when she pulls it down, I see an Imagine Dragons T-shirt.

There are so many questions slamming into me. I want her story. Want to know if her parents kicked her out because she's gay or if she couldn't go to them, but then I don't want to push either. And I don't want her to think that's all there is to her so instead of saying that, I tell her, "Imagine Dragons are so badass. What's your favorite song?"

She looks shocked at first and then she tells me. I tell her my favorite, and she starts reciting lyrics and asking me about other bands. She tells me she can play the guitar and that she wants to be in a band one day. I tell her I play basketball, but it's not what I want to do. That I don't know what exactly that is yet, but I have time to figure it out.

We talk for almost half an hour. TJ and the others might be wondering where I am right now, but I sort of feel like talking to her is more important. So I keep doing it. Here and there she lets little things slip. She was kicked out. Her siblings are at home with her family. It's when TJ steps up behind us that her conversation cuts off. TJ notices and tries to leave, but it's too late. Tammy pushes to her feet and starts to walk away.

"Be right back," I tell TJ. Jogging, I catch up to her. "We can still talk."

"No. I'm sure you want to leave with your boyfriend."

I kind of love that she realized I'm with TJ. "He doesn't mind. It's because of him I'm even here. He's cool."

But she just shakes her head. I don't know why she felt okay talking with me but doesn't with TJ. He's like this beacon that everyone follows. For whatever reason, though, she chose me. "Hold up. Don't go anywhere, okay. I'll be right back."

I grab paper and pen from TJ before going back to Tammy. I write down my name, number, and even my mom's name and number. "If you ever need anything, or even if you just want to talk, you can call me, okay? I hope you call. I'd like you to call. My mom... she knows I'm gay. She'd make sure we could help with whatever you need. Or if you just want a friend, or whatever."

I tense for a second when she throws her arms around me. Tammy squeezes me tightly, and whispers in my ear, "None of my friends wanted to talk to me when I told them I'm a lesbian. I didn't even know anyone else who was gay before I got kicked out."

If I had a different mom, I could be her, or something like her. Life is such a gamble, you never really know what hand you'll get. We should be thankful for the things we have. "TJ was my first friend who is gay. I didn't think I needed any, but now I'm glad I have him. That I have more than just him."

Tammy pulls away. "Thank you."

"Don't lose my number. The top one is home. You can call collect if you need to."

She smiles, nods, and walks away. When TJ's arms wrap around me from behind I lean into him. "Your eyes are open." It's what I told him I wanted. What I just thought to myself I was achieving, and now he sees it too.

"Yeah... yeah they are."

"Go somewhere with me?" TJ asks.

"Sure. Where do you want to go?"

He replies, "A bridge," and even though I'm not sure what he means, I follow him.

We find Amy and Lisa to tell them good-bye. Amy hugs me and whispers, "He is so fucking into you." When I pull back she must be able to see the shock on my face because she laughs and then kisses my cheek.

"Amy." I reach for her arm, but she just winks and then walks away, with Lisa right behind her.

"What was that?" TJ asks.

"I'm not sure." I just know I hope she's right.

When we get into a cab, TJ tells the driver we're going to the George Washington Bridge. He's quiet for most of the drive over, which feels like it takes forever. I don't look at my cell the whole time, so I'm not sure if it really does or not.

"Over there." TJ points. "The south sidewalk is the only one open so you can walk it." His small camera bag bumps around between us as we make our way to the bridge.

"I swear to God, I think my nuts are going to freeze off. We're definitely coming back when it's warmer." Being close to the water definitely doesn't help the temperature.

The bridge is freaking huge, though. Cars speed each direction, but for some reason the noise doesn't take away from the coolness of it. You can see the whole city from here.

We stop when we get to the middle. TJ's still being more quiet than usual. "A flash mob isn't going to jump out, and you're going to ask me to marry you or something, is it?"

TJ grins. "Nah, you'll totally be the one to propose." He moves over and stands next to me, both of us looking over the bridge. After a minute, he takes out his camera and snaps a few pictures before putting it back.

"It's crazy how much world there is out there," I say, not sure why I need to fill the empty space.

"I don't understand it," TJ whispers, his voice nothing but sadness, emptiness, almost like Shaun before we parted. My stomach drops out.

"Get what?" I step closer.

"Why people care… why it's such a big deal. Did you know a guy committed suicide up here? He was gay and tortured so bad at school that he thought the only way out of it was to jump from the George Washington Bridge. What the fuck is that? How can people treat someone so badly that they jump off a fucking bridge? How can they kick their kids out or make them live the way Shaun does? I just…." He shakes his head. "I don't fucking get it, and it makes me so mad!"

My hands shake because this isn't like TJ. He always has it together. He's the levelheaded one, and I'm usually the one freaking out. "Hey." I box him in with my arms as I hold on to the railing, so close to him I feel the heat of his body. "That's why we're doing this. That's why *you're* doing this. You're going to show people it's okay. You're going to help people who feel alone."

I'm not used to this kind of thing. I don't know the right thing to say, but there's never been a time in my life that I wanted the right words to come more than I do now.

"I just don't get it. Why do people think there's something wrong with us? Why are we supposed to hide, and change and lie, what? So they'll love us? So they won't disown us or kick us out. So we don't have to go to places like we went today just to get food? So we don't feel so bad about ourselves we have to jump off a bridge? Fuck. I can't believe I'm crying." He wipes his eyes, and then I pull his hand away. "Kiss me or something so I chill out. I don't know why I'm losing it."

Getting close to him, I grab his face in my hands. "Kissing you is going to make you chill out? I would have thought the opposite."

"Yeah." He frowns. "Good point."

I get serious again because I think he needs to hear it. And there's a part of me who wants to give TJ all the things he's given me. "Sometimes it's just overwhelming. We all need to lose it. Or if you're like me, you lose it every day."

He gives me that eye roll he does that says he thinks I'm crazy, and then smiles.

"You're doing something important here. Something that matters. Remember that."

"*We're* doing it," he says.

"Because of you."

I look up at the spikes in his hair. As though he can read my mind, TJ pushes mine off my forehead like he always does. "We're gonna be okay when we go back home, yeah?" he asks.

Home. I almost forgot we're going back tomorrow. My stomach rolls a little. Not because I don't think we'll be good but because I want to stay. This has been like a dream, like escaping reality. When we get home, I have to figure out how to create a new reality. "Yeah. We'll be awesome. I...." *Am a total wuss....* "I think I'm... falling in love with you, or whatever." That came out totally wrong.

Shaking his head, TJ chuckles. "I think I'm falling in love, or whatever, with you too. Minus the whatever." TJ pauses a second and then steps back. I watch as he unties one of the bracelets on his wrist. "Gimme your arm, Bradley."

Without a word, I hold it out to him. TJ pushes my sleeve up. His fingers fumble a few times and then he ties the string bracelet on my wrist. "I'm a film guy." He shrugs. "I like cheesy movie moments. This is ours."

I suddenly really, really like cheesy movie moments too. "Thanks. Do they mean anything? The bracelets?"

"Nope. I just like them. Guess that means I like you even more."

My insides are sizzling in the best possible way. This time, I do what he said a few minutes ago. I lean in and kiss him, in the middle of the George Washington Bridge.

We're not quiet as we walk back. Not quiet as we wait for a cab. Not quiet as we ride back to the hotel because we always seem to have something to talk about. As we're lying in bed that night I want to tell him to *minus the whatever* too but before I get a chance, TJ falls asleep. Tomorrow, I'll tell him. We always have tomorrow. Until then, I close my eyes, my fingers tracing over the band on my wrist.

Chapter 32

WE'RE DRIVING to Ohio so we can go back to the secondhand store. We'll stay a night at the hotel we were at before and then head back home the day after. We've been playing stupid games where we recite a movie line and the other person has to guess the movie. TJ kicks my ass every time, but considering he's like a movie-ninja, it's not like I expect anything else.

"We're playing basketball when we get home," I tell him when we're almost to Columbus.

"Okay." He shrugs. "I'll find a way to beat you at that too, even if I have to cheat."

I make sure he notices when I roll my eyes. "Yeah right. You couldn't beat me."

"Even if I cheated?"

"How would you cheat?"

TJ glances my way. "I used to play football when I was younger."

I watch him, waiting to see where he's taking this change of subject.

"I was alright at it. Pretty good, actually, but I didn't love it. My dad hated that I didn't love it. He didn't understand how I couldn't love it. He doesn't get the film thing at all."

"That sucks." I slide my feet down from their perch on the dashboard. "I bet he'll get it after this, though. He'll see that's what you're supposed to do…. This documentary… it's going to be awesome." I don't even have to see the finished product to know that. I witnessed it, and I know I'll never forget it.

"It's definitely not just another gay movie." He winks.

"I've never seen a gay movie."

"Holy shit, we totally have to change that, sports guy. When we get home we'll lock ourselves in your room all day, and I'll make you watch all my favorites."

I'm thinking that sounds like a really cool day. "Okay."

There's a pause before TJ says, "What about your friends? Things aren't going to get weird?"

Even though I wish it didn't, my stomach rolls a little. "No. They know I'm gay. They always have."

"Yeah, but you also were a dick to me in front of them, even though they knew, and you lied to your best friend about being with me. It's like you try to protect them from seeing it."

Dude. Why is he bringing this up now? I put my feet back on the dash. "That was before. You know things are different now." It's not like I haven't apologized. It's not like I don't already feel like a jerk.

TJ sighs. "I wasn't trying to make you mad. I'm just bringing up the truth. I was pissed when you treated me like crap at The Spot that day. I wouldn't just be pissed anymore. I'd be hurt. I just…. Tell me the truth, okay? It's easy to say when we're in New York or anywhere else, but it's different at home. If you're not sure you can do it, I want to know up front."

TJ pulls off the freeway. Without replying I watch a bit of the city go by. I get it. It makes me feel like a pussy that he even has to bring it up, but it's not like I don't get where he's coming from.

He stops at a gas pump and kills the engine. "I'll get the gas."

Before he can get out I grab his arm. "I want to do this. And I already told them I'm with you now. I'm not going to say I'll never screw up, but I won't hide this. I want it." Which should be obvious since I said I want what we have twice. I always ramble and overkill when my nerves start going haywire like they are now. "I won't lie to you. Or to them about you."

He stares at me all serious for a minute, and then with a huge smile on his face, TJ leans over and kisses me. It's over way too quick, his mouth gone almost as soon as he touches mine.

"Want anything? I'll grab us some drinks and stuff, pay for the gas, and then we'll get on the road again."

"I'll take a Mountain Dew," I tell him, and then TJ climbs out of the car. I watch him until he disappears into the store.

Flickers of our conversation spur me to pick up my phone and text Chase.

I was a dick. Shouldn't have lied. Be home late 2morrow. Wanna chill?

The reply comes back almost immediately. *I'm down.*

That's always how Chase and I have been. We fight, and then we're just over it. It's way easier than talking about it forever like my mom always wants to do.

My fingers shake as I type my next words. *Not 2morrow but later in the week I'm gonna bring TJ to the spot with us. He's cool. You'll like him.*

No reply, no reply, no reply. My stomach feels heavier and heavier as I watch my phone. Minutes tick by. Chase doesn't text. TJ doesn't come out. It seems like it's taking him a long time in the store, but I still can't take my eye off my phone. Why isn't Chase texting back? *He's not going to be okay with it. He's going to think it's too weird. I won't be able to hang out with my best friends....*

I actually freaking jump when a ring breaks out in the SUV. It's not my phone so I lean over and grab TJ's cell from between the seats. "Mom" lights up on the screen. Quickly, I glance out. He's still not coming. If she's anything like my mom she'll freak out if he doesn't answer. Mom assumes the worst so I hit talk. "Hello?"

"Thomas?"

I sort of glance at the phone as though that will explain why she called him Thomas when he said he always goes by TJ.

"No, this is Bradley. I'm the one doing the documentary with him. He's in the store real quick. I just didn't want you to worry. I can go grab him for you."

For some reason my heart is hammering the way it does when I'm about to get yelled at by Mom.

"You're doing the documentary with him? Was it your idea? He knows how I feel about this. It's not what he was supposed to be working on, while on this trip!"

Wait. "What? I'm not sure what you're talking about. We're doing TJ's film documentary for school."

"The documentary about being gay. That's unacceptable. Put my son on the phone, please." Her please is issued more like a *now.*

Turning toward the door, I see TJ standing outside my window. He sees me on his phone, his lips stretching into a frown. His face going hard.

He pulls open the car door, looking pissed. I don't know what he has to be so mad about. "Dude. Your mom's tripping out." I cover the phone, hoping she won't hear.

"Mom," TJ says when the phone is to his ear. She yells so loud I can hear her.

"This is not what you were supposed to be doing, Thomas Joseph! You told me you would put this nonsense behind you!"

TJ's face goes pale. He starts backing away, but we both know it's too late. He knows I heard. He's not supposed to be here—or at least not supposed to be doing *this*. His mom isn't okay with any of it. His mom isn't okay with him being gay.

Holy shit. My heart is hammering and my stomach turns.

TJ's been lying to me the whole time.

Chapter 33

FIVE, TEN, fifteen, twenty minutes pass, and TJ doesn't come back. With each minute, my skin gets tighter, my mind thinks of more questions, my body temperature rises. There are so many different things going on inside my body, I'm not sure which of them to focus on.

Twenty-five, thirty, thirty-five. Finally TJ gets into the SUV. He tosses his phone down. I wait for him to explain or say *something*, but he stays silent.

"What the hell?" I blurt. "She doesn't know we're here?"

"She knows we're here. She just didn't know *why* we were here. Well, at least she didn't know why before, but now she does. She does pay close enough attention to realize I've been gone." His jaw works as though he's grinding his teeth.

I open my mouth to say something else, but TJ cuts me off. "I don't want to talk about it. She canceled the credit card. There's enough money on a debit for gas to get us home, but that's all." More to himself than me, he mumbles, "I should have fucking known when the card wouldn't work." But then he snaps out of it, opens the door, and says, "I'll fill up for real this time."

My thumbs start doing their drumming thing. I'm confused about what's going on. This is such a huge part of who TJ is. He's out, and proud, and people accept that about him, yet he lied about this? About his parents being supportive? It doesn't make any sense. It's not who he is.

He fills up the gas tank and then climbs back in. Without a word he starts changing the navigation in his phone, I'm assuming to point us home.

Words play a pickup game on the end of my tongue, yet none of them make it out. Why would he lie about something like this? And if he lied about that, what else hasn't he told the truth about?

Over and over I flip my phone in my hand. Each time it's face up, I check for a text from Chase that isn't there. I think about TJ and the fact that this whole trip could have been a lie.

My body wars with itself, not sure if anger or hurt should win. Right before the call, he asked me to always tell him the truth, yet he'd never given any of it to me. The more I think about it, the more pissed I get. And why the fuck isn't Chase texting me back? I mention TJ, and he goes off the radar. I mention TJ, the guy who's been lying to me, and piss off my best friend.

"Dude—"

"Not now. I said I can't do this right now." TJ's movements are sharp as he stabs the plug into his iPod and turns on music.

My hands tighten into a fist. I wish I could punch him. My hands itch to do it.

Hours pass by in silence except for TJ's music. Eventually, it starts raining. Perfect. That matches my mood. My eyes drift closed, but I'm too upset to fall asleep. Stupidly, I hope he'll try to wake me up, try to talk to me, but he doesn't. When I finally open my eyes again, the rain has stopped. We're the only car on the open road, fat, gray clouds in the sky… and a rainbow.

There's a voice in my head that wants me to take this as a good sign, but that's ridiculous. Everything is screwed up, and a few colors in the sky won't change that. I wish they could. If things hadn't gone down the way they had, I can see TJ mentioning the rainbow, having some kind of story about one, or saying how it's the perfect end to our trip.

We still don't talk.

It gets dark, and even though I'm pissed I say, "You should let me drive. You've been at it forever."

"I got it" is the only reply I get, so I let it go.

The only time my phone beeps is when I get a text from Mom checking on me. I tell her we'll be home tonight instead of tomorrow, that TJ needs to get home. The longer we go in quiet, the more pissed I get.

When we stop for gas the next time, I don't say a word to him. Just get out of the SUV, take a leak, grab some food, and then get back in to wait for him.

It's after one in the morning when TJ pulls up in front of my house. We've been on the road for over fourteen hours.

He doesn't turn the engine off, both of us sitting there without moving. My body is stuck between anger and hurt. I don't want to feel either of those things, don't want this to be a big deal, but it is. He made me believe things, and now I don't know if any of them are true. I wanted to be with him, when I'd never wanted to be with anyone else, and for all I know, none of what he said is real.

"You lied" is all I manage to say. I don't want to be like this. Don't want my gut to ache. If this were Chase, he wouldn't give a crap. He'd move on. He probably would have been the one to lie. Not me. I fell for the first gay guy I met.

"I know."

I wait for TJ to say more, but he doesn't. He leans forward, pressing his head to the steering wheel.

The whole time I hear him cutting me off, think about the fact that I pissed off my best friend because I wanted to be with him. That I made all these changes because he made me think they were the right thing, but really he's a bigger liar than I am.

"You told me not to lie to you when you were doing it to me." These words make me feel weak. I shouldn't. *Get out of the car, go inside, and forget I ever met him.* Yet I don't move.

"It's different, Bradley. You don't…. It's not like you never lied."

My pulse slams in my ear. My hands tighten into a fist again. "At least I admitted my shit. You played the part like you had your crap together but really you're even worse than me. Was any of it true?" I never pretended to have all the answers like TJ did.

Another pause. *Say something.* The second the thought goes through my head I'm even angrier at myself than I am at TJ. I shove the door open, and I wait. Get out of the car, and wait. Close the door and then open the back. As soon as I grab my bag, TJ says, "Bradley…," but then doesn't continue. I slam the door shut, and without looking back, I'm gone. It's probably better anyway. Chase still hasn't texted back, and I'm not going to screw things up with a friend for someone who was never even real with me.

Chapter 34

EVEN THOUGH I got home late, I get up for school the next morning. If I stay Mom will ask me eleven thousand questions about the trip and TJ that I don't want to answer right now. Maybe never.

"Are you sure you don't want to stay home?" she asks me as I finish my cereal. "You have to be tired, kiddo."

"Nah, I'm good. I wanna catch up with the guys. I'm gonna run over and tell Chase I'm back so he can ride with me."

I make it to the door before I hear, "Bradley?"

Shit. "Yeah?" I say without turning around.

"Everything's okay, right? If you need to talk, I'm here."

I'd pretty much rather do anything than talk to my mom about a guy. It's not her, she's cool, but no one wants to talk to his mom like that. "I'm fine." I smile at her. "I just got back from a road trip with no adults. How could I be anything but good?"

Mom chuckles. "Crazy boy. I want details when you get home. And tell TJ when he gets it all put together, I'd like to see the film."

My stomach drops out at that. I won't get to see the documentary now. I have no idea how it will turn out. It's something I should have thought about last night. Now that I am, it makes the anger root even deeper inside me. "Yeah. Sure. Gotta go."

Chase's mom answers when I knock on the door. She's in a business suit like she always is, ready to head out the door. "Bradley, we haven't seen you for a while. I hope everything's going well."

I don't take offense to the fact that she didn't realize I was gone. It's even possible Chase told her I'd be out of town. Things always go in one ear and out the other with his mom. She's a realtor and works even when she's not working.

"Hey, Mrs. H. Have a good day." She steps out of the house, and I step in calling out, "Chase. Get your ass down here." The best way to do things with him is to pretend nothing happened. If I do, then he will, and we'll go on like we've always been. That's what works for us.

He looks over the railing of the stairs, wearing a pair of jeans and no shirt. "You're back early. Let me finish getting dressed. Text Jabbar and tell him not to pick me up."

Just that easy I know things will be fine. Yeah he might not have texted back after I mentioned bringing TJ around, but that's obviously not something I have to worry about now anyway.

The next few days are just like they've always been on the surface. The four of us chill at school. They ask about the trip, and I tell them the cities we went to, but that's basically it. That seems to be enough for them. Jabbar asks me once if I'm with TJ. He's still with the girl he met before we left. Jabbar, Chase, and Marcus's eyes are all on me waiting for my reply. The table is quiet, and I wonder how they'd react if I said yes. But I'm not with him, so I say no. Jabbar teases me about when I'm ever going to get laid. Everyone laughs, including me, and then the conversation goes off onto something else. Inside, I'm dying.

On my third day home I'm sitting on the couch, flipping through my phone. TJ hasn't texted or called. My fingers toy with the idea of sending him a message. What if he got into trouble? What if he can't make our documentary?

Obviously he doesn't want to talk to me about it, though. We rode in a car together for half a day and he didn't say a word.

Mom jogs down the stairs giving me an excuse to toss my phone to the coffee table.

"What ya up to?" she asks.

"Not much." I shrug.

When the couch dips and she sits beside me, I know I'm in for it. "You were having a blast when you were gone, yet you've been home for three days now and haven't said a word about the trip. I let it go, giving you time, but you know how impatient I am. And how nosey." She nudges me. "What happened, Bradley?"

It's times like this I wish we weren't close. That she wasn't a kickass mom who told me to go on a road trip with a guy. Not many parents would be that cool.

"Did you…?"

"Seriously." I groan. "Can we not do the sex thing again? I didn't have sex, and if I did, I probably wouldn't be bummed about it." Totally a fact.

Mom sighs. "I know this isn't comfortable for you. I'm sure this is hard for you to talk to me about at all. You're dealing with things I might not be equipped to handle, but I love you and I'll find a way. Whatever you need, Bradley. If it's not me, we'll find someone. If it's not sex, which I'm okay with by the way, I know there's something. We're a team, you and me. You gotta pass me the ball for me to help you score."

I let out a loud laugh.

Mom's face turns bright red. "I was trying to relate by using a basketball analogy! Forget my use of the word score in this conversation." It's the first time I've seen Mom's face so red, and I kind of love her for it. Love the fact that she's laughing about it, and that she cares enough to try.

"You're cool, Mom."

With a mom-smile on her face, she looks at me. "I try."

But no matter how cool she is, I can't really talk to her about this. Not most of it at least. "The documentary was awesome. I think... I don't think I'll ever be the same." It's the one thing I'll take out of this trip. "I'll talk to you about all of that soon. And the other stuff... it's too weird. It's not you. It's just.... TJ wasn't who I thought."

She gives me a sad nod. "We all get our hearts broken. It doesn't matter if you're gay or straight, remember that. The heart is universal, Bradley. We love the same and we hurt the same. We have to have those experiences. I'm sorry if you got hurt, but I'm proud of you for putting yourself out there enough for it to happen. That makes you very brave."

Brave. That's not a word I've used to describe myself in a long time. I would have been lying to myself when I used the word before. When I came out, I was being "brave," but I really wasn't. I just wanted it to look that way. That's not enough for me anymore, though.

"Hey... that place you told me about? For gay teens, or whatever it is? I think... I think I wanna go." I started to find myself on our road trip, maybe it's time I go all the way.

"Okay." Mom puts a hand on my leg. "Okay. I'll call them and see what we have to do." Her eyes are a little wet, and before she makes mine the same, I stand up and hug her.

"I'm gonna go do my homework." I make it to the bottom of the stairs before something stops me. Part of me is annoyed with myself for wanting to say what I do, but then, it's the truth. Regardless of what happened, I know it's true. "Whatever went down with me and TJ... it wasn't all his fault." I don't know why he lied, but then, I don't know why I lie sometimes either. Fear, maybe. I get that, even though I'm still upset about it. "He has issues, but he's a good guy."

"I'm glad. And so are you."

I know I want to be. And I want to believe the best about TJ too.

Chapter 35

IT'S CRAZY the things you see about yourself if you really look. I get pissed at people for things I see in myself, for things I do myself. I judge people, so I think people judge me. If I'm gay, they're going to think I'm this or that, and maybe I am or I'm not, or maybe people will think I am or they won't. It really doesn't matter.

We take our strength where we can get it like Matt does. With him it was makeup, which I still don't understand, but I don't have to. He does it for him, not me or anyone else.

I can't expect people to be a certain way or think that because things go a certain way for me, they will for everyone, the way Richie believes.

Dave and I have been talking in the five weeks that I've been home. It helps. I know more gay teens and adults than I ever have, since I started meeting up with them, but it's different with Dave. I know him, and I can trust him. He's the only person who knows everything that's gone down with TJ.

TJ who lied to me, the way I lied to Chase, and have lied to myself. We all have something to hide. Sometimes it's right and sometimes it's wrong. Sometimes we have a reason and sometimes we don't, but that doesn't change that we've all done it. Some of us feel like we have to—like Shaun. I guess it's possible TJ did as well.

I've walked away from things I want, things I love, like Greg did, only I've also tried to walk away from who I am. In the past five weeks, I've thought of all the things I regret, and I don't want to keep adding to that list.

As I sit on Chase's porch, waiting for him to get home, I replay the discussion we had at the LGBT group meeting last night. The group that I've been going to for weeks that my friends don't know about. It was about words and the power they have, both positive and negative. How important it is to use them but that we have to own them too.

I figure it's time I use some with Chase.

His dad is out of town on business, which means Chase is using his car. I'm only here about ten minutes before Chase pulls into the driveway.

"What's up, bro." He bumps his fist with mine as he sits by me on the stairs. "What ya doing?"

I let the first thing that comes to mind out of my mouth. "Why didn't you text me back that day?"

He raises one of his brows at me. "What day?"

"The day I got home from the road trip. We were texting, and I told you I wanted to bring TJ around and you never replied."

"I wasn't home. Then my phone died. When I got home I went to bed, and right after I woke up in the morning, you were at my house. Did you miss me or something, Collins?" He smirks, and I suddenly feel like an idiot. That's something I need to work on too—not automatically assuming the worst.

"I thought you didn't reply because you didn't want me to bring TJ around…."

Chase starts popping his knuckles. "Why would I care about that? I mean, he seems kind of different than us, but if he's your boy, then he's your boy. Not that kind of boy. I mean, it's okay if he's *that* boy, but I didn't mean *that* boy. I just meant—"

Even though I try to hold it back, I start laughing.

"Fuck off, Collins. I'm trying not to screw this up."

I appreciate that. I'm glad he cares enough, but it's still funny. "Sorry. I'm used to being the one who rambles when I don't know what to say." When I settle down enough, I look at him more seriously. "You said it would be weird. To see me with someone, I mean."

Chase shakes his head. "I say a lot of stupid stuff. And in a way it would be, but that's because I'm not used to it. I've never seen it. You said you're gay, but sometimes it's easy to forget since you've never hooked up with a guy."

And in reality, I can't be mad at him for things I've thought about myself. "That's because it felt like it would be a little weird for me too. I'm gay. I know it. I don't see what you do when you look at a girl, but… well I guess I had to get used to it too."

Chase starts drumming his thumbs on his knees. I never realized he did that like I do. "It's like in a way, I don't want you to be gay. Maybe that makes me a dick, but we've always done everything the same. You're my best friend. It pisses me off sometimes because I just want you to be like me. I want you to go out with us when we go out with girls, so I'm probably a jerk about it. I shouldn't be. I'm trying not to be. And if anyone else had a problem with you, I'd kick their ass. It's just… you're my boy. It's almost like, you've got this thing I can't be a part of."

Whoa. I didn't see that coming. It's probably the most words Chase has strung together without any kind of sarcastic comment in his life… and I get it. I've felt the same about him, Marcus and Jabbar. I've felt like they have this thing between the three of them that I'll never be a part of. It makes sense for Chase to feel it too. His parents always have so much going on that he's not involved with, but when it's come to the four of us, Chase is always the center of it. When it came to being my friend, Chase was always the most important.

"I'm sorry," I tell him.

"Not your fault."

"You'll always be my best friend. Always." As close as we are with Jabbar and Marcus, I know it might not always be that way. Shit happens, and people grow up and pull apart but not Chase and me. I just didn't realize he felt the same.

"Always." The top of his fist comes down on mine, and then I do the same for him. "We're gonna tear shit up when we go to Cali next year."

I laugh, pretty sure he's right. Ever since freshman year, we knew we wanted to go to college there.

"For sure." After waiting for a second, I say something else that's been on my mind. "I need you to quit saying fag or calling things gay. I know you don't mean it like that, but it's hard for me to hear."

Chase nods. "Yeah… that's stupid. You're right. Sorry. That guy… TJ… you're into him?" he asks. He's sort of wringing his hands together, obviously a little nervous, but still, he's saying it because he's my friend. Because he's trying.

"Yeah." I look at the ground. "I thought I'd be over him by now, but I'm not."

Chase pauses a bit before continuing. "Then you should get him back, or whatever. You and Jabbar are all in love and shit." He laughs.

"I can't wait till it happens to you. I'm going to talk so much crap."

"Nah, player for life," he teases. From there we talk school, and this summer, and college next year. I tell him a little about the road trip and some of the things TJ and I did. The more I talk about it, the more I think about TJ. About who he is… about his parents not being supportive and how much that must kill him. The more my mind is with him, the more little things start making more sense—the sadness I often sensed under the surface, that night on the bridge. TJ was hurting. The whole time he was hurting, and I didn't know. No matter what, he was always there for me, though.

I don't want to risk losing him the way Greg lost Darren. I want to fight how Stacy and Michelle fought for Layla because they loved her so much.

Pushing to my feet, I hold my hand out for Chase. "I gotta go. There's something I need to take care of."

Our hands slap together, and then I'm heading to my car, texting TJ as I go.

Chapter 36

I WAIT for thirty minutes in the parking lot of The Spot.

He's not gonna come, he's not gonna come, he's not gonna come.
It's all I can think, but then I see a familiar SUV drive into the parking lot. My lips pull into a smile making me realize how much I really do want him to be my boy. Not in the way I am with Chase, Jabbar, or Marcus. I want him to be my boyfriend again—for real this time. But who knows if he even wants me? It could have all been some kind of game for him.

I jump out of my car, and open the passenger door to his as soon as he parks. "Wait. Let's get out," he says. TJ leans against the outside of his SUV, and I do the same, next to him.

"Did you get into trouble when you got home?" I ask him. It's not what I came to say, but it feels pretty neutral.

"Nope. What are they going to do to me? Take my car? The credit card? They know I don't give a shit about things like that. The only reason I even used the card is because I needed it for the trip."

He still hasn't looked at me. I want his eyes on me, but I'm still angry too.

"But hey, at least my dad knows I'm really gay, and it's not going to change. That's a plus, I guess." He shrugs.

The statement brings back every reason I'm upset with him, all the reasons I'm confused. "You told me they both knew, and that they were okay with it. Why did you lie?"

For the first time since we got out of the SUV, he turns my way. "Did you ever think I was embarrassed? That I lied because I wanted it to be true so fucking much? Pretending it was true made it easier to the point that I almost believed it? Why would I want to tell people my own parents wouldn't accept me for who I was?" he asks.

"I didn't realize I would fall for you. The first time we met, I just thought you were this good-looking jerk who wasn't proud of who he was, just like my parents weren't okay with me. I wanted you to see that there's nothing wrong with who we are. That other people are okay with it. I wanted…." He shakes his head. "I wanted to make them proud. If I made this awesome movie, if I showed them that we're just like everyone else. If I showed them the things we go through just to be who we are, that it would make them okay with who I am."

Guilt starts slamming me into the ground.

"And your mom is so awesome. The more I heard about her, I just… it made it hard. I wanted that. Then, the more I got to know you, the more I liked you. I wanted to make you okay with who we are. I wanted you to see that maybe it was okay to like me too because I really fell for you. As the trip went on, the more you changed, the more I fell for you. The longer it went on, the harder it became to admit the truth."

Each of his words collides into my chest—they engrave themselves into my mind, and heart. Just like me, like so many of us, TJ needs to know it's okay. That we're okay. This guy who accepts everyone for who they are, and respects every person he meets, who just wants us all to be the best people we can, needs to know there's nothing wrong with who he is. That he's accepted. That he's loved.

TJ sighs before he starts talking again. "When I came out, Mom was okay with it. Not happy, but she accepted it until I told Dad, and he didn't approve. I'm Thomas Joseph Bennett the third. Bennetts aren't gay. Not our Bennetts. So I told him I was confused. That he was right, and that he'd never hear of it again. See, I get so pissed when people hide who they are, when they aren't proud of it because even though I lived out with everyone else in my life, I hid from my parents. I wasn't really pissed at you for being scared. I was angry with myself."

He always seemed so together, and in a lot of ways he was, but in others, he hid more than me. "TJ—"

"Bennetts may not be gay, but we do succeed," he says. "I guess I thought if I won this contest, if I got entered in the national, that they'd be happy. Maybe then they'd be proud. Maybe I could change their minds. Stupid, right?"

He turns away again, but I reach out and hold his face so he can't. I struggle to find all the strength TJ showed me out there on our road trip. "There's nothing wrong with who we are. Especially not you. You're the best person I know." My hand slides away from his face, down his arm, and I latch his hand with mine. At home, at the place where everyone I know hangs out, where anyone can see us.

"Suck-up." TJ smiles, but it doesn't reach his eyes.

"Tell me you know how awesome we are."

His smile gets a little bigger. "I do. I really do. I think I learned it on the trip right along with you. You weren't the only one with your eyes closed. We both have them open now. I hoped my parents would too, but what can you do?"

I tighten my hold on his hand. "I'm sorry. I... I didn't get it."

"I would have told you, sports guy. I promise I would have told you. The bridge... I almost did it that night, but I freaked."

Before he even finished speaking, I start shaking my head. "I know. I'm not mad. I think... I think in a small way, I used your lie for an excuse. I told Chase I wanted you to meet him, and then he didn't text. I was worried about that. Being with you was easier when we weren't home, and I was stressed out about what people would think, and so I latched on to your lie as a reason not to have to step up."

Neither of us is perfect. No one is. I think everyone in this world is a liar one way or another, until they decide not to be, at least. I'm owning that, and I'm changing it. TJ is as well.

It only takes a few steps for me to be standing in front of him. His legs are spread slightly so I can stand between them.

"What are you doing?" TJ asks.

"Trying to tell you to minus *the whatever*."

"Huh?" He knows what I mean. I see it in his eyes.

"I want you to be my boyfriend. I wanna take you to prom because I don't give a shit what anyone else thinks. And I don't need *the whatever* anymore. I know how I feel."

"Dude, all the guys will be so jealous," he says not for the first time. "My boyfriend is not only a hot basketball player, but he's sweet too. I won't tell anyone the last part if you don't want me to." His smirk has stretched into a full-on smile now.

"That's cool and all, but are you going to say it back? I totally just put myself out there," I tease him.

TJ leans forward. As soon as his mouth touches mine, I open my lips for him. He tastes me, and I taste him, and yeah, I don't think I'll ever get tired of kissing him.

He leans his forehead against mine. "No boners in public."

"You still haven't said it." I pretend to pull back, but he stops me.

TJ grins. "I love you too." And then he fingers the bracelet on my wrist. "You kept it."

"Didn't take it off once." This time, it's me with the big smile. It's awesome to hear that, but I want more. "Can you go get the documentary? I wanna see it."

He rolls his eyes. "Shut up, Bradley. Like I didn't put it in my SUV when you called. Meet me at your house."

He follows me over, and I don't care if Chase or anyone else sees him here. As it happens, they don't. He's not home, but Mom is, and she gives me this embarrassing wink when we walk in.

TJ and I go upstairs to watch the documentary. My eyes don't leave the screen the whole time. When Matt and Henry speak, I remember how I felt when I first saw Matt. How at that time, I still wasn't so sure about this whole thing. My chest aches when Shaun's altered voice tells us how alone he feels. I think of how much Dave has been there for me when he and Richie are on screen. With each interview we watch, I'm going through the emotions again. It's incredible. I can't believe he did it. When I tell him, TJ says, "We did it." Just as the credits roll, I see the proof right there.

The History of Us created by TJ Bennett and Bradley Collins.

"Here. I need to show you something else." TJ gets on his laptop and starts another video. A video of me. But it wasn't video when he took it.

"How?" I ask, but then I remember what he told me that first night about film frame and how he could take different still images and put them together to create a moving picture. There are images I don't remember, pictures I didn't know he took, and others I did. They start from the morning we met with Matt and Henry—shots in the car, in Ohio, the abandoned building, after Jeff and Greg's, the picture we took together in Central Park, and the end, the rainbow I saw on the open road, when we were driving home. This is my film frame turning into my moving picture. The picture of me being okay with who I am. In my whole life, I've never been as proud of that person as I am at this moment.

Epilogue

"DUDE. YOUR tie's all screwed up. Let me fix it." I start messing around with TJ's tie, but I'm obviously making more of a mess than anything else.

"You got the bow tie. I should totally be the one rocking a bow tie. What are you doing to it?" He teasingly pushes my hand away.

"Move, boys. I'll fix it." Mom steps between us and straightens TJ's tie, then mine. "Very handsome young men." She gives me a thumbs-up, and I roll my eyes. As long as she doesn't slip me condoms, we'll be good.

My brother laughs as Mom drags us outside to take a million pictures. Jabbar, Marcus, Chase, and their dates are supposed to pick us up in the limo at any minute. TJ and I will head to prom with the six of them.

This won't be the first time my friends officially meet TJ as my boyfriend. We've hung out quite a bit, but this will be the first time he's at my school, where everyone else can see. It doesn't bother me at all. I was a little nervous when I got the ticket for him. Chase and the guys said if they gave us shit, we'd have our own prom, but no one did. And I know they won't tonight either. If they do, screw them.

I still think about Shaun and wish he was able to think *screw them* too. TJ and I tried to contact him a couple times, but he won't reply back.

Mom has taken about ten million pictures before she finally stops. She's hanging out in the yard waiting for Chase and the guys to get here before we start all over again. TJ and I stand on the porch stairs when he bumps my arm. "Hey. Did I tell you I heard about the documentary?"

My heart beat picks up. "Shut up. Tell me." He knows he hasn't.

His eyebrows rise. "We did it. It won and now it goes to national. My advisor at Hollywood Film School is stoked. He said the board is impressed." He shrugs. "It was the extra incentive I needed. I got in."

I knew he would. He's too good not to, but it still makes me feel like I'm flying. We'll both be in California next year. "You did it. I can't believe you fucking did it!"

"Brad!" Mom shouts from where she's standing in the yard, obviously not happy with my language.

The limo pulls up saving me. The guys and their dates get out.

"*We* did it," TJ reminds me, then leans over and kisses my cheek. I hear the camera snap from Mom, and my friends all start whistling and yelling. Me? I'm still flying, totally settled in and happy to be who I am.

NYRAE DAWN can almost always be found with a book in her hand or an open document on her laptop. She couldn't live without books—reading or writing them. Oh, and chocolate. She's slightly addicted.

She feels a special pull to characters in their teens. There's something so fresh and fun about the age that she adores exploring. Her husband says it's because she doesn't want to grow up. She doesn't think that's such a bad thing. Luckily for her, he doesn't either.

Nyrae gravitates toward character-driven stories. Whether reading or writing, she loves emotional journeys. It's icing on the cake when she really feels something, but is able to laugh too. She's a proud romantic, who has a soft spot for flawed characters. She loves people who aren't perfect, who make mistakes, but also have big hearts.

Nyrae is living her very own happily ever after in California with her gorgeous husband (who still makes her swoon) and her two incredibly awesome kids.

Find her online at:
Blog: http://www.nyraedawn.blogspot.com
Facebook: https://www.facebook.com/nyraedawnwrites

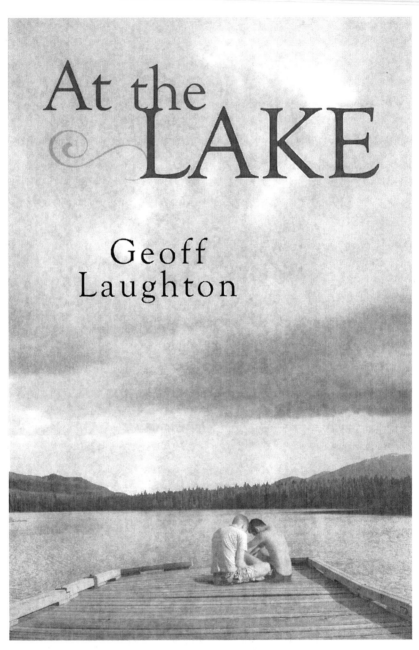

At the LAKE

Geoff Laughton

http://www.harmonyinkpress.com

The
BOOK
of
ETHAN

RUSSELL J.
SANDERS

http://www.harmonyinkpress.com

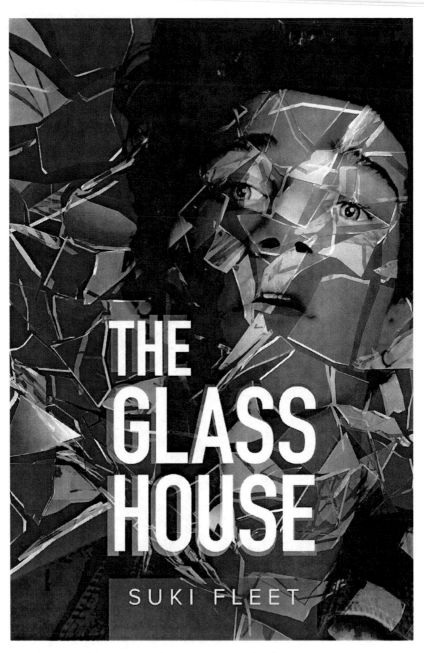

THE
GLASS
HOUSE

SUKI FLEET

http://www.harmonyinkpress.com

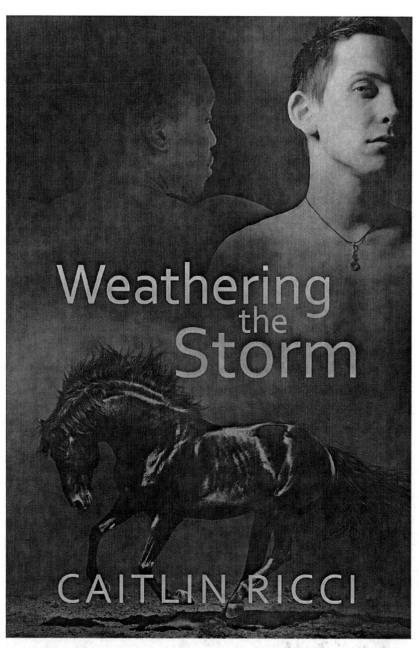

Weathering
the
Storm

CAITLIN RICCI

http://www.harmonyinkpress.com

CPSIA information can be obtained at www.ICGtesting.com
Printed in the USA
LVOW10s0402130216

474949LV00022B/325/P